ALIVE UNTIL I DIE

STEVE TAYLOR

STEPHEN TAYLOR BOOKS

CHAPTER 1

After taking a big sniff, Danny jerked his head away fighting the urge to gag as he screwed the lid back on the gone-off milk. He'd arrived home after running a security team at an exhibition centre in Birmingham. It was late and the drive home had been slow and arduous. All he wanted to do was have a cup of tea and hit the sack. Dumping the bottle in the bin, he grabbed his jacket and took the five-minute walk to the mini-market on the high street. Pushing the door open, he threw up a wave to the guy behind the counter.

'Alright Tam. Your dad's got you doing the late shift again then,' chuckled Danny as he continued towards the fridges at the rear of the shop.

'Yeah, tell me about it. The perks of being the owner's son,' Tam shouted back.

'It's tough at the top, mate!' Danny yelled, bending down to pick up a four-pinter. When he straightened up his eyes fell upon the curved mirror mounted on the back wall of the shop. It was there so the shop assistant could see kids mucking about down the aisles or shoplifters tucking bottles of booze into their jackets. In this case, Danny could see a stretched image of the front window and what looked like a super-wide pickup truck reversing towards it, fast. Before he could turn to see it properly, the front of the shop imploded in a shower of shattered glass, followed by the horrific screeching of the aluminium window frame being torn away by the vehicle's bodywork. The pickup thudded to a halt when it hit the shop's cash machine. Its casing was dented but it held fast on its bolts to the floor. Before the dust could settle, a figure dressed in black climbed in through the debris waving a sawn-off shotgun around. Danny bobbed down below the eyeline of the shelves. The gunman turned his ski-masked head in Tam's direction.

'Do as you're fucking told and you won't get hurt,' he said with a hateful snarl.

As Tam shook with fear, the sound of a screaming petrol engine filled the air. Like a scene from The Texas Chainsaw Massacre, a second member of the gang jumped in through the dust wearing a hockey mask. Holding a screaming disc grinder he went to work on the bolts holding the cash machine to the ground. As he lit the front of the shop up in a shower of white-hot sparks, a third member of the gang appeared in the back of the pickup truck. He fixed chains around the cash machine, ready to winch it on to the flatbed as soon as they cut the last bolt.

'Listen up, you've got sixty seconds to open the safe your old man has out back. Now move,' said the first guy, jabbing Tam with the shotgun as he pushed him towards the stock room.

'Ok, ok. Please don't hurt me,' Tam pleaded.

Seeing them move away from the two working on the cash machine, Danny moved around the shelves to get closer. He picked up a tin of plum tomatoes, frowning as he felt the weight. Putting the tin down, he looked along the shelf. Moving left, Danny picked up a family-size tin of new potatoes. Bobbing it up and down in his hand he smiled to himself, satisfied. Standing so he could draw it back like a pitcher ready to throw a fastball, he kicked the bottles of wine off the shelf besides him. The gunman turned at the clinking bottles rolling down the aisle. Before he could react to the sight of Danny's head above the shelves, the heavy tin came hurtling across the shop like it was rocket propelled. It caught him edge-on right between the eyes, flattening him to the floor in one swift movement. Shocked and bewildered, Tam stood frozen to the spot. It took several gestures and mouthing from Danny before the penny dropped and he slid into the stockroom, locking the door behind him.

Bobbing back down, Danny moved to the unconscious man and picked up the dropped shotgun. Breaking it open he checked the two cartridge ends sitting in the barrels and clicked the gun shut again. At the front of the shop, the grinder's screaming petrol engine dulled down to a popping tick-over as the last bolt disintegrated under its cutting disc. The guy in the back of the truck immediately started to winch the cash machine up the tailgate.

'Oi, dickheads, drop everything and get down on the ground!' shouted Danny emerging from behind the newspaper stand, the barrels of the shotgun darting between the man on the truck and the guy with the grinder.

In a surprise move, the guy on the ground screamed the petrol grinder's trigger to the max and hurled it at Danny. It hit the floor with a horrific clang, its cutting disc sparking on the concrete as it dragged its way towards him. Trapped in the narrow aisle, Danny backed up as fast as he could and let the approaching grinder have it with both barrels of the shotgun.

3

The noise was deafening in the confined space. The blast blew the grinder into the shop counter where it embedded itself and stalled. When the smoke cleared, Danny spotted the grinder guy jumping into the truck's cab and firing it up. He lurched the truck forward with the cash machine swinging half-on and half-off the back. Dropping the empty shotgun, Danny ran forward and launched himself at the back of the truck. He grabbed the chains around the half-on and half-off cash machine as the truck accelerated down the road. With his trainers dragging on the tarmac, Danny pulled himself up and over into the back of the truck. His feet hit the metal surface wide, keeping low to steady himself against the erratic driving.

A blow caught him heavily across the cheekbone, knocking his head to the side. He looked up slowly to see hateful eyes looking at him from behind a mask. Danny's face hardened, the muscles in his cheeks tensing as he gritted his teeth. His eyes narrowed, the pupils dark and burning as his anger grew. The masked guy moved to kick him off the side of the truck, Danny went down on one knee. Absorbing the blow to his side and wrapping his arm around the attackers leg. Holding it tightly Danny powered a punch to the guy's balls before standing up and swinging the man around, pitching him off the side of the truck. He landed arse-first through the windscreen of a parked car and lay unconscious, folded up across the front seats.

Seeing a corner coming up, Danny jammed the winch in reverse, dropping the cash machine crunching and sparking onto the tarmac. As the truck cornered, the cash machine swung wide, hooking around a lamp post like a ship's anchor. The truck jarred from thirty to a halt in a split-second, sending the driver crashing through the windscreen and Danny flying over the top. He crashed through the hedge of the house opposite and rolled across a soft

4

lawn. He lay there for a while checking for broken bones. When none presented themselves, he stood up to the sound of sirens approaching and strobing blue lights reflecting off the buildings.

Why does this always happen to me?

CHAPTER 2

Walking briskly from his office in Whitehall, General Rufus McManus turned into Marsham Street. He moved through the public with an air of disdain, his back straight and head up in a parade ground manner. He may have been in a Savile Row suit, but he was still a general, a leader of men, protector of the crown. He got to his destination and with a flash of his identification, entered the modern metal-clad facade of the Home Office building. Checking his watch for the time and picking his wallet and change from the metal detector's tray, he made for the meeting room. He had made sure he was early; he wanted to be first in, prepared and ready for the fight.

'Good morning, Rufus,' said the Prime Minister and his Minister for Defence, William Pringle.

'Oh, er, good morning, Prime Minister, William,' he said taking his place around the conference table. He placed his file on the table and sat back, calm on the outside but fuming on the inside at being caught off-guard.

They sat patiently until the official time of the meeting

approached and two more members of the Security Council arrived.

'Good morning, Hector, Howard,' they said in unison.

After the pleasantries, the Prime Minister opened the meeting. 'Gentlemen, let's get right down to business, shall we? William, if I may, over to you.'

Rufus eyed the Minister for Defence with contempt. The man was an idiot, a people pleaser. He moved through the government offices telling politicians what they wanted to hear, rather than what should be said.

'Yes, of course, Prime Minister. Continuing on from our last meeting and my analysis of the data on the UK's terrorism threats, it is my opinion that we can no longer support the General's Project Dragonfly.'

'That's a pile of horseshit, William. You couldn't successfully analyse your own bloody desk, let alone the ever-growing threats to this country. Project Dragonfly already has six top-level threats under investigation, including the theft of 200 prototype rifles and military body armour. All these pose a clear and present threat to the security of this country,' said Rufus, his face flushed as he leaned in and glared at the minister.

'General, may I ask you to refrain from such outbursts,' said the Prime Minister with a warning look.

'Sorry. My apologies, Prime Minister, but I would like to know how Mr Pringle expects to tackle these extreme threats without the resources of Project Dragonfly,' said Rufus, managing to cap his temper.

'We have perfectly good resources covered by our intelligence services, not to mention the covert intelligence services provided by Howard,' said William, shooting his answer back with a look of triumph towards Rufus.

'I strongly disagree. My assets are highly trained for anti-terrorist response which is not something they train the Secret Service for,' said Rufus looking at Howard for support.

'Howard, have you any comment to add?' said the Prime Minister looking across the table.

'To a certain extent I'm inclined to agree with the General. I have a certain number of resources outside of the Secret Service to tackle extreme threats to the country. But I believe the General's Project Dragonfly has a valid place in this country's protection,' said Howard matter-of-fact, without emotionally taking sides.

'Thank you, Howard, I think we'll leave this for now. William, I would like to see a full report on your proposed replacement of Project Dragonfly within our existing intelligence services. And General, I would suggest that you bring some positive results to the table next time we meet.'

'Yes, Prime Minister,' said Rufus.

The meeting ended and the members dispersed one by one. Howard moved beside Rufus as he prepared to leave.

'I just wondered, how's the investigation into the stolen rifles and body armour going?' said Howard moving in front of him.

'We have one or two leads, nothing concrete at the moment. And you?' said Rufus, both men being cagey as men of secrets always are.

'Mmm, we're looking into the possibility that the robbery was executed by paid professionals. Mercenaries, to be precise,' said Howard, searching Rufus's face for signs he was already aware of the fact.

'Well Project Dragonfly is already looking at all possibilities, so if you have information you wish to share, we will be happy to take it from here, ok?'

'Certainly. You'll be the first to know of any developments,' lied Howard as the two men shook hands and departed.

Outside, Rufus marched his way back towards his office. As he rounded the Houses of Parliament, he received a text.

He's one of Howard's.

Deleting the message straight away, Rufus ducked into a nearby mobile phone shop and paid cash for the cheapest phone they had. Typing a number from memory, he sent a message.

Get rid of the new boy.

As soon as he got a tick to say it had been read, he casually tossed the phone over the railings into the Thames and continued along the embankment.

CHAPTER 3

The Toyota Land Cruiser hurtled precariously down the country lane, its driver leant forward, concentrating hard to see the corners through the drizzly night sky. He swore as he clipped the verge, bouncing off it in a cloud of grass and mud. He let out a sigh of relief as the dirt track came into view. Sliding the 4x4 off the road, he gunned it down the track and skidded to a halt next to the rented farmhouse. Turning the engine off, he opened the door and stood searching the darkness for telltale signs of danger. Satisfied, he hurried indoors, taking the stairs three at a time. Grabbing a large canvas bag, he threw it on the bed, turned and grabbed a file with a classified stamp on the front and tossed it in. Thirty seconds later he'd filled the bag with money, his passport and clothes for a few days. Leaving everything else, he went back downstairs into the dark lounge. Leaving the light off, he dumped the bag on the table and stood at the window. His eyes scanned the darkness outside. Pulling his phone out with shaky hands, he scrolled through the contacts and tapped Aunty

DANNY PEARSON WILL RETURN

For updates about current and upcoming releases, as well as exclusive promotions, visit the authors website at:

www.stephentaylorbooks.com

ALSO BY STEPHEN TAYLOR
THE DANNY PEARSON THRILLER SERIES

Snipe

Heavy Traffic

The Timekeepers Box

The Book Signing

Vodka Over London Ice

Execution of Faith

Who Holds the Power

Alive Until I Die

Sport of Kings

Blood Runs Deep

Command To Kill

No Upper Limit

Leave Nothing To Chance

melted into the darkness of the woods. The figure watched Tripp for a moment longer as he drifted away, before turning and disappearing into the darkness.

CHAPTER 4

Parking in his reserved space, Danny trudged to the front of the three-storey Victorian building. Ignoring the lift, he bounded up the stairs with a little less enthusiasm than usual. Yawning, he pushed through the squeaky oak doors of Greenwood Security.

'Had a heavy night, have we?' said the receptionist.

'You could say that, Lucy. Is he in?'

'Yes. Mr Jenkins is in with him,' she said with a smile and a lingering look.

'Thanks,' Danny replied, seeing her blush when she realised he'd noticed her looking. He smiled and wandered off through the desks to his office with its sign on the door: *Danny Pearson, Director of Operations.* He put his jacket on the coat stand, checked his messages, then went to the office next door and knocked below the *Paul Greenwood, CEO* sign and entered.

'Morning all,' he said.

'Morning, Daniel. Edward was just filling me in on your night's entertainment,' said Paul, sitting back in his chair.

'Mmm, there wasn't anything entertaining about it. Thanks for getting me out of there, Ed. I knew having a friend who's Chief of the Secret Intelligence Service would come in handy one day. I swear, if I had to listen to one more stupid question from that idiot detective, I would have staged a breakout of my own.'

'How the hell do you get yourself into these predicaments?' said Paul shaking his head.

'What? It wasn't my fault! I only went out for milk,' said Danny with a chuckle.

'Alright, at least you're ok. You know we have to get the schedule and team sorted for the sheikh's personal protection detail today,' said Paul, turning back to business.

'Already on it, boss. I'm going to use John's team now they're back from Germany.'

'Ok, good choice,' said Paul.

'Right, I'll leave you to it. Thanks again, Ed. I owe you one,' said Danny leaving the office.

Sue walked along the river path near Sawbridgeworth train station. Her black Labrador Toby trotted off the lead beside her, sniffing and zigzagging across the path as things caught his eye. She continued along the path, oblivious to all around her as she complained about her job in a ping pong text conversation to her sister. In a gap between the incoming messages, she looked up and realised Toby wasn't behind her. She called his name and backtracked when he didn't come. Calling him again, she heard a bark from behind the bushes at the water's edge.

'Toby, what are you doing?' she said pushing through the undergrowth.

When she came out the other side, Toby was dancing

excitedly back and forth barking at the water. Looking down at the river, Sue recoiled at the sight of a body in the reeds at the water's edge. The skin was pale and waxy and lifeless eyes stared straight up from below a bullet hole in the middle of the forehead. Her feet slipped on the wet grass as she panicked and dragged herself back through the bushes to the path. As Toby looked up lovingly, his tail wagging, excited and proud of his discovery, Sue stood in shock, dialling 999 with shaky hands. When the operator answered she burst into tears, dropping to her knees. A short time later the area was swarming with police. They closed the path and taped the scene off ready for the forensic team. Officers Bale and Spires stood at the top of the path near the station road. A few curious locals had congregated on the bridge over the river, trying to see what was going on. Chinese whispers changed the gossip as it worked its way along. Some said a woman had been attacked, others favoured a suicide, and a few were sure they'd found drugs.

'The rubbernecks are out in force today,' said Bale, nodding in the bridge's direction.

'Yeah, call off the detectives, I bet they've got it all figured out by now,' said Spires already bored with path-guarding duty.

The sound of sirens broke the monotony and seconds later three plain black cars came into view speeding down the hill towards them. Turning off the sirens and flashing blue lights hidden behind their grills, they pulled up along the bridge. Two dark-suited men got out of the front car and two more out of the rear car. The large Range Rover in the middle sat there, the privacy glass giving no hint to the occupant.

'Hello, who's this lot?' said Bale as the men approached down the path.

'Who's in charge?' said the front guy, his voice short and his face serious as he shoved MI6 ID in their faces.

'Detective Inspector Grey, sir. He's down near the body,' said Spires.

The agents ducked under the tape and continued along the path. Two stopped twenty yards from the officers and stood guard while the other two continued to the crime scene. They approached Grey, MI6 IDs already out and displayed.

'Agent Harris. I just need to view the body.'

'Be my guest,' said Grey, stepping out of his way as he gestured towards the river.

Harris pushed through the bushes, emerging on the riverbank next to the body. He stared at Tripp's body for a while before taking his mobile out.

In the back of the Range Rover parked on the road, a mobile rang.

'Yes.'

'It's him, sir. Tripp. Shot in the chest and head.'

'Thank you, Harris. Lock down the site and get rid of the local plod. We'll take over from here.'

'Yes sir,' said Harris, hanging up.

The man in the back of the Range Rover made another call.

'Edward, it's Howard. We've found Tripp's body.'

'Damn. The bastards. What do you want to do?'

'In his last call he said they are planning something else. He also said we have a leak in the department. We'll have to go outside the agency. Meet me at the club later, we'll talk then,' said Howard, hanging up. He sat for a moment deep in thought before looking at the driver's eyes in the rear-view mirror.

'Downing Street please, Frank, I need a word with the Prime Minister.'

The car pulled quietly away, heading back towards London.

CHAPTER 5

After copious cups of coffee, the schedules for the sheikh's visit were all sorted. Danny sat back and yawned, happy that the weekend was only an hour away. His mobile went off, snapping him awake. He smiled at the caller ID.

'Scotty boy, to what do I owe the pleasure?'

'It's Friday night, old man. I was thinking you, me and the Minelli twins, a meal at The Ivy and a party at mine,' said Danny's best friend Scott Miller.

'Who the hell are the Minelli twins?'

'The Minelli twins are a pair of rather lovely personal trainers from my private health club. Very fit, very flexible and very keen to meet you,' said Scott like an excited schoolboy.

'Can't we do it another night, mate? I was up most of last night and I'm knackered,' said Danny logging his computer off and grabbing his jacket off the back of the chair.

'Absolutely not, dear boy. You do not turn the Minelli

twins down. When you see them, you'll know why. Shake off the pipe and slippers, old man. I'll pick you up at seven,' said Scott, refusing to take no for an answer.

'Ok, ok. I give in. I'll go home and freshen up and see you at seven. I'm not doing an all-nighter though,' said Danny on his way out.

'Good man, I'll see you later,' Scott said hanging up.

Danny popped his head round Paul's door.

'I'm off now, Paul,' he said to his boss and friend.

'Ok, have a good weekend,' Paul said waving him off with a smile.

'I'll let you know on that one. Scott's taking me out with the Minelli twins,' Danny said raising his eyebrows.

'Who are the Minelli twins?'

'I have absolutely no idea. See you Monday,' Danny said over his shoulder as he wandered out of the office.

———

A small walk from the Houses of Parliament, behind a subtle Georgian façade, lay Britannia Gentlemen's Club. Other than a small brass nameplate on the heavy black door, there was no evidence of the club within. You couldn't just join the Britannia, you had to be introduced by a member and then approved by a board. Edward Jenkins passed the black iron railings and hopped up the white steps to the front door. Noting the CCTV camera above him, he rattled the door knocker. It opened immediately, and an immaculately suited man gestured him into a large hallway.

'Good evening, sir, how may we help you?' said the suited man, closing the door behind him.

'I'm here as Mr Howard's guest,' said Edward,

knowing the secret government agent was only ever known as Howard for his first or last name.

'Certainly, sir, may I take your coat?'

'Yes please, Mr...?' asked Edward taking his jacket off as a younger man appeared from nowhere to take it off him.

'Jarvis, sir. This way, if you please.'

Edward followed Jarvis through a sitting room full of high-backed leather chairs and Chesterfield sofas, through a dining room full of high-flying businessmen and politicians, finally leading him into a smaller oak-panelled dining room with half a dozen private dining booths. When they reached the corner booth Edward saw Howard sitting relaxed at the table.

'Edward, punctual as always. Please take a seat,' said Howard, gesturing for him to sit.

'Would you like a drink, sir?' asked Jarvis as Edward slid in opposite Howard.

'I'll have a scotch on the rocks please,' said Edward.

'And you, sir? Would you like another?'

'Same again please, Jarvis,' said Howard.

Jarvis returned with drinks and took their food orders. Howard waited patiently, watching him leave before he started his conversation.

'Quite a mess, isn't it?' he said.

'That's an understatement. Has Tripp's family been informed?' said Edward, taking a big swig of scotch.

'Yes. The official line is, he was killed on a training exercise. They'll be looked after. The river incident never happened. I have issued police and press a gagging order and told them it's a matter of national security,' said Howard pausing as the food arrived.

'What about the informant?' said Edward once the waiter had left.

'Or informants, dear boy. Someone sold Tripp out and supplied detailed information about the body armour and Pentic rifles. The stolen weapons and body armour were on a need to know basis under the MoD's research and development department. We could be looking at someone on, or with access to, the National Security Council.'

'What are we going to do about Benton, pull him in?' said Edward, picking at his food, his appetite vanishing.

'No, he and his friends are way too careful. We only have Tripp's last report saying he'd made contact, and we still have no idea who the buyer is. Losing the body armour is bad enough, but if we don't get the 200 prototype rifles back and they fall into the wrong hands, we could have a major international incident on our hands and an enormous embarrassment for the government. No, we need to get another man on the inside, someone who has no active links to the agency or MoD.'

'Who do you have in mind?' said Edward, half-knowing the answer.

'I want to use Pearson. He's off everyone's radar and he worked with Benton back in the SAS.'

'I don't think he'll do it,' said Edward, looking Howard straight in the eye.

'Oh, he'll do it,' said Howard with a small smile.

'What makes you so sure?'

'Let's just say he owes me for a Chinese takeaway,' said Howard, thinking back to how he'd cleared up the mess after Danny blew a Chinese assassin's brains out for killing his girlfriend, Kate.

'If he agrees, we'll have to keep him off-grid—nothing official, no paper chain.'

'I agree. I think we should bring in Thomas Trent and John Ball to run operations. Danny knows them and they're off the books. It would be safer that way,' said Howard, finishing his dinner.

'Good idea. Until we find out who leaked Tripp's cover and the MoD files, the more unofficial the better.'

CHAPTER 6

The big Volvo XC90 4x4 turned off the quiet B-road a mile or so from the small village of Chipping Ongar, Essex. It drove slowly down the long dirt track, its headlights illuminating the hedges that lined either side. Eventually the car bumped up onto a concrete surface that ran into the middle of a horseshoe-shaped collection of farm sheds. Commander Rex Benton pulled the car up next to a plain white 7.5 tonne lorry. The place looked deserted, but Benton knew better. He turned off the engine, plunging the courtyard into moonlit darkness. Stepping out, he stood listening for a few seconds while his eyes accustomed to the dark. Satisfied, he walked towards the large sliding door of one of the barns.

'Everything quiet, Mendes?' he said into the pitch black beyond the building to the left.

'Yes boss, I've just been out to one of the perimeter sensors. Bloody fox set it off,' said a figure appearing from the shadows in full black body armour and balaclava. He was armed with a new stubby Pentic carbine rifle in his grip and a Glock 17 holstered on each hip. Miguel Mendes fell in behind Benton as he slid the door open a couple of feet, letting a wedge of light from within reflect off the car and truck.

'Boss,' said a tall, sandy-haired guy in jeans and a jumper.

'All the cargo loaded on the truck, Knowles?'

'Yes boss.'

Benton turned his attention to a smaller, wiry man engrossed in an indestructible looking field laptop, showing pictures from four night cameras and boundary sensors.

'You ok, Kristoff?' Benton said.

'*Da*, is good. The cargo plane will land around 1 a.m. The fixer has all the customs documents and consignment paperwork. He'll meet us at South Mimms services for the exchange.'

'Right, Mendes, you get the cameras and sensors, then get changed into civvies. I want all our kit bagged and in the Volvo in thirty minutes. When Mendes gets back, we clean the place down and take everything: trash, cups, even the bog roll. Leave no trace. We're not coming back here. Ok?'

'Yes boss,' they all said in unison before all moving into action.

Turning his back to the men, Benton moved to the table against the far wall. He folded a map of Surrey, then picked up a set of aerial photos. He was about to tuck them into a leather case along with building blueprints and a manila folder with a red classified stamp across the front, when his right hand trembled uncontrollably. Dropping the paperwork back on the table, Benton grabbed it with his left and held it tight. He stood still as vivid images filled his mind, evil people, tortuous people, as clear as they'd been when they were flesh and blood. Pain flared as phantom electrical pulses brought their torture back to reality.

'We still need someone to replace Dennis for that one, boss,' said Peter Knowles, moving up beside him.

Benton glared at him with wild eyes, seeing the image of his nightmares instead of Knowles. He moved his hand toward his gun, letting it drop to his side at the last minute as the fog lifted and the figure of Knowles imprinted on his mind. 'I know, Peter, we'll have to be more careful after Tripp.'

'Has the client said anything about Tripp's investigation?' said Knowles, noticing the strangeness of Benton's reaction but not having the nerve to challenge it.

'He doesn't know; local plod's off the case. The spooks moved in and took over, and not MI5 or his guys in MI6. Come on, let's bag it up,' said Benton, moving off with the case.

Less than an hour later Kristoff and Mendes sat in the lorry, with Knowles in the passenger seat of the Volvo. They sat patiently for Benton as he inspected the storage shed for anything they missed. He worked his way slowly from the back wall, wiping all surfaces and handles and chairs for a second time with a heavy bleach-soaked cloth. Just before he reached the sliding door, he spotted a cigarette butt on the floor. He picked the stinking, cheap Russian cigarette butt up and placed it in his pocket.

Bloody Kristoff and his cigs.

After wiping the handle and sliding door, he took the keys to the property out of his pocket and wiped them down before throwing them inside and sliding the door shut. The place was rented under a false name and paid up for three months. The agent would keep the deposit when they couldn't contact anyone and think nothing more about it. He climbed into the driving seat of the Volvo and headed off down the dirt track with the lorry trundling along behind him.

'Call the fixer, tell him we'll meet him at South Mimms in forty minutes,' he said to Knowles.

'On it,' said Knowles, already dialling the number.

The phone was answered, but nobody spoke.

'ETA forty minutes, blue Volvo, white truck,' Knowles said.

The phone clicked as Hamish hung up.

'He give you the silent treatment?' said Benton.

'Yeah,' replied Knowles.

'He's a very cautious man, Mr Campbell,' said Benton, turning onto the A414 towards Harlow.

They drove reservedly, keeping to the speed limit as they made their way onto the M11 and then the M25, eventually taking the slip road off at junction 23 for South Mimms services. Benton slowed round the roundabout, letting the truck move up close behind him as they entered the services. They drove to the far corner of the car park and parked up side by side. Within seconds of stopping, a grey Ford Focus started its engine. It drove through the car park and pulled up beside the Volvo. A pale, nervous guy with mop of copper-coloured hair and a matching bushy beard looked over at Benton and gave a little nod. Benton reciprocated. Both men remained where they were, studying and scanning the car park for anything out of place. Eventually Hamish got out with a large brown envelope in his hand. Benton lowered the window as he approached and took the envelope from him. Hamish turned immediately without a word and got back in his car. By the time Benton wound the window up, Hamish had started the car and was driving away.

'A very cautious man, Mr Campbell,' Benton repeated as he turned the interior light on and checked the documents.

'All good, boss?' said Knowles.

'Yep, give them to Mendes. Tell him to meet us at the unit in Slough after he's loaded the plane.'

Knowles took the envelope and got out. When he got back in, Benton pulled away. He didn't wait for the truck; it was going on a different route to them.

CHAPTER 7

The sun streamed through the wooden blinds in Scott's spare room. Danny opened one eye, squeezing it shut again when the intrusion of daylight set a thump off in his head. He repeated the process a few seconds later, reaching over to his old G-Shock watch sitting on the bedside table. Half eight. He rolled on his back and tried to clear the fog out of his head.

What the hell did I drink last night?

To his surprise, the duvet beside him moved and the attractive face of a Minelli twin rolled into view. Her sleepy eyelids opened to show off her soft brown eyes. She smiled with a row of perfect white teeth at Danny's surprised look.

'Don't worry, you were the perfect gentleman. Very drunk, but still the perfect gentleman. You were going to sleep in Scott's recliner chair, but I said you could share the bed.'

'Ok. Er, right. Sirena, right?' said Danny, embarrassed.

'Yes, Sirena. Marie disappeared with Scott, who I think might have been less of a gentleman than you,' she said, rolling back the other way as Danny got out of bed, thankful to find he still had his underwear and T-shirt on. Finding his trousers on the floor, he hastily pulled them on.

'Nice bum,' she giggled as he slipped out the door.

After splashing his face with cold water and running his fingers through his mop of unruly hair, he wandered through to sounds of movement in the kitchen.

'Morning, old boy. You look rough. Top night, what?' said Scott, chuckling as he clicked on the kettle.

'When I start to remember any of it, I'll let you know. What the hell was in those drinks you kept buying?'

'I think it would be easier to ask what wasn't in them,' Scott said, throwing him a packet of paracetamol from a kitchen cupboard.

'Thanks, mate. Why don't you look like a train wreck?' said Danny curiously at Scott's fresh as a daisy look.

'Oh, I went onto non-alcoholic cocktails halfway through the night. I didn't want to get to drunk, after all, I had the lovely Maria to look after,' said Scott with a grin like a Cheshire cat.

'You bastard, you could have told me,' said Danny, taking a cup of coffee from Scott, and swilling down a couple of headache tablets.

'Where's the fun in that, old boy? You were enjoying yourself so much I didn't want to spoil the fun. I haven't seen you let your hair down that much for years.'

'Mmm, fair enough, it was a good night,' said Danny, managing a smile despite his head. He could never stay angry at Scott, they'd been friends since school.

'So, how was the lovely Sirena?' said Scott, looking at Danny with raised eyebrows.

'She was very nice and nothing happened, ok?'

'What an absolute shame,' Scott said, his floppy hair bouncing as he turned his head and beamed at the Minelli twins wandering barefoot into the kitchen, redressed in last night's sparkly dresses and carrying their high heels in their hands.

'I've called a cab,' said Maria, moving closer to Scott and pulling him in for a passionate kiss.

'Are you sure? I could take you home, my dear.'

'No, it's ok, I'll call you later,' she said, kissing him again.

Sirena moved up to Danny and kissed him on the cheek. 'If you want go out again, call me. I might let you act like less of a gentleman next time,' she said, sliding her phone number into his shirt pocket.

She walked off with her sister, leaving Danny slightly red-faced. When the door shut behind them, Scott laughed out loud.

'Don't say a word,' said Danny smiling back at him. He was about to say something else when his phone rang. He picked it up and frowned at the ID.

'Paul, what's up?' he answered.

'Sorry to disturb your Saturday but something's come up,' Paul said, the tone of his voice serious.

'Ok, what is it?' said Danny, his curiosity piqued.

'Not over the phone, can you come into the office?'

'Er, yeah. I can be there in about an hour and a half.'

'I'll see you then,' said Paul, ringing off.

'That sounded serious. You'd better have a bacon sandwich before you go,' said Scott pulling a frying pan out of the cupboard.

Danny looked at his watch. 'Can you drop us at the office afterwards?'

'Of course, dear boy.'

'In that case, get the bacon on, mate,' grinned Danny.

CHAPTER 8

The old Russian Ilyushin Il-96T cargo plane hummed into Serbian airspace on its planned flightpath to Istanbul airport. Its pilot and co-pilot checked the maps and dials for its four Aviadvigatel jet engines. When the GPS reached a certain position, the pilot wound back the engines and started gently descending. He gave a nod to his co-pilot and pressed the comms button for his headset.

'Istanbul, this is KD1200, we have a hydraulic failure. Requesting a divert to nearest Serbian airfield, Lisičji Jarak.'

'KD1200 this is Istanbul air traffic control, please stand by.'

They waited in silence for a few minutes before the radio burst into life.

'KD1200 this is Istanbul air traffic control, your request is granted. Lisičji Jarak airport has been notified and is expecting your arrival.'

'Thank you, Istanbul. KD1200 over and out.'

Punching in the co-ordinates for the new airport, the pilot banked the plane around and continued his decent to Lisičji Jarak airport.

———

Fifty miles away, a beaten-up, old, navy blue truck pulled up to the security gate at the airfield. The guard had been paid well and knew they were coming. He raised the gate without the truck having to stop. It drove noisily off towards the rear of the airfield, past the hangers and light aircraft, to park up on a large concrete pad.

The airfield was small and quiet, primarily used for learner pilots, small aircraft owners and crop sprayers. Only two people worked in the control tower and both of them had been paid to turn a blind eye once the cargo plane landed. They didn't have to wait long before a hum of jet engines preceded the view of the plane as it dropped through the clouds. It came in low over the airfield fence as it needed all the short runway to stop. A puff of grey smoke plumed off the tyres as they kissed the tarmac, the planes flaps right up, air braking hard. It slowed and turned at the end of the runway, finally pulling to a stop close to the truck.

When the jet engines wound down, the pilot lowered the rear loading door. The driver's door of the truck swung open and Gregor Krulsh climbed down. At six-foot-six and 250 pounds of muscle, he wasn't someone you forgot. He slammed the door with a shovel-sized hand, the rough, faded, blackish blue prison tattoos on display as a warning to all. He turned his clippered, crew cut head towards the plane and gave a nod to the co-pilot standing on the loading ramp.

The passenger got out of the truck, a shorter middle-aged man, grey-haired and portly around the middle. He looked less intimidating than Gregor, but with a face looking like someone had chiselled it out of solid granite, he still looked like someone you didn't want to mess with. He went to the rear of the truck and lowered the hydraulic lift while Gregor walked over to the plane and went inside. Moments later he emerged, guiding four large wooden crates down the planes ramp on an electric pallet loader. Dropping them on the tar mac, Gregor wheeled the pallet loader on to the truck lift and raised it. After a bit of moving about he emerged out of the truck, guiding a pallet with four boxes of washing machine parts that matched the consignment paperwork from London for customs in Istanbul. He pushed them into the plane and strapped them down. When he'd finished he turned to the pilot and co-pilot. They looked nervous as his ice-blue eyes tore into them. He reached into his jacket, causing them to flinch, and brought out a large envelope. As he handed it to the pilot, he held it tight, leaving the pilot holding the other end not knowing what to do.

'You will never speak of this, now go. I was never here,' he said in a low menacing growl.

The pilots stood trembling slightly as Gregor let go of the package and walked out of the plane. Minutes later Gregor had the pallet loaded on the truck and was driving out of the airfield as the plane's cargo door closed behind them and its engines hummed and wound up in power.

'Lisičji Jarak, this is KD1200 requesting clearance to take off.'

'KD1200 you are clear for takeoff.'

As the plane climbed to cruising altitude on its way to Istanbul, the co-pilot opened the envelope and flicked his thumb through the wad of money.

'Istanbul, this is KD1200. The hydraulic fault has been fixed and we are resuming our flightpath to Istanbul airport.'

CHAPTER 9

Feeling decidedly more awake, Danny waved Scott off outside Greenwood Security. He jogged up the stairs, enjoying the surge of blood pumping through his heart and the warming of his leg muscles. He pushed the old oak door open and entered the office, only breathing slightly heavier than normal. It was Saturday and the lights were off and the desks empty. Over on the far side of the office the conference room door was open. Paul appeared in the opening.

'Lock the door behind you please, Daniel,' he said, moving back out of sight into the room.

Danny turned back and flicked the latch. With the feeling he wasn't going to like what this was all about, he made for the open door.

His feeling was proved right when he saw Howard sitting at the top of the table with Edward Jenkins to his right and Paul to his left.

'Whatever this is, the answer's no,' Danny said remaining standing, his face hardening as his eyes burned angrily.

'Can we dispense with the theatrics, Daniel? And for Christ's sake sit down,' said Howard in his usual matter-of-fact manner.

Reluctantly, Danny dragged the chair out slowly and slumped down without comment.

'We have a situation that requires your particular skill set and I'd appreciate your co-operation. I'm sure I do not need to remind you that you are in my debt,' said Howard, knowing he had the upper hand.

'Ok, ok. Just get on with it,' said Danny, his face as dark as his mood.

Edward opened a file in front of him and spread three blown-up photographs on the table in front of him. Reaching in, Danny picked up the first picture of the front of a farmhouse with a car in front of it. The walls and windows were torn to bits with great lumps of brickwork blown out and cratered. The car's metal skin had ripped into sharp shards, the impact so great it had shattered the aluminium wheels.

'Mmm, looks like a 50-calibre by the destruction. But the entry holes are too small. Maybe 6, 7mm, they shouldn't have that power,' Danny said, putting the picture back down and looking up at Howard for answers.

'They were made by a prototype Pentic carbine high-velocity rifle with new 6mm tungsten carbide armour-piercing rounds. It's very light, very accurate, and twice as powerful as a C8 carbine. It is one of a shipment of 200 destined for field testing at Hereford, stolen two weeks ago from a secure facility in Essex.'

'What about the barbecued guy?' Danny asked, looking at the other two pictures.

'The burnt gentleman is Dennis Leman, ex-SAS soldier. He left the regiment three years ago. We believe he did a stint as a mercenary for the Sudanese government before returning to Britain. That's all we know about him, until an armed guard put a stray bullet into an oxygen storage tank while Mr Leman and co. were stealing the Pentic rifles. The resulting explosion blew Mr Leman to kingdom come while his colleagues escaped,' said Howard, picking up on Danny's growing curiosity.

'The CCTV from the robbery shows a tight group, professional soldiers, Special Forces formations, in and out quick and clean. We ran all ex-Special Forces operatives through the computer and came up with three names that matched height, build and age. Funnily enough your name came up top, followed by Nicholas Snipe who we know is deceased. The final name was Commander Rex Benton,' said Howard, pausing to note Danny's reaction to the name.

'And the stiff? Danny said, tapping the photo of Tripp from the morgue.

'He was one of ours, Sergeant Simon Tripp. Knowing the unit was a man short, we sent Tripp in undercover to find Benton and work his way into the group. All was going well until someone in the department sold him out. Tripp was making a run for it, but as you can see, he never made it.'

'I don't understand, why don't you just pick up Benton and his crew?'

'Because, dear boy, there are several complicating factors. Benton and his team didn't dream this up by themselves. They are following the orders of someone, and this someone is powerful enough to have influence in MI6 and access to MoD information,' said Howard, with an out of character hint of anger noticeable in his voice.

'I served with Rex Benton on my first tour of Afghanistan. He was a damn good soldier and a good friend. What happened to him?' said Danny, pushing the photos back to Howard.

'His unit were all killed by ISIS when a mission went wrong. Benton was taken and tortured for three months before he escaped, and walked for forty miles barefoot out of the badlands. He was never the same after that. Feeling abandoned by his country and blaming himself for his unit's death, he left the SAS. We only have sketchy reports after that, ending in the Sudan where we believe he met Dennis Leman.'

'And the rest of his gang of thieves?' said Danny, still unimpressed.

Howard pulled out two photocopies of MoD personnel files, complete with a photo in the top corner.

'Commander Rex Benton you know. The other gentleman is Peter Knowles, an ex-Navy SEAL with a clean record,' said Howard. He slid over a military report written in Spanish with a picture of a short, stocky Mexican on the top.

'Miguel Mendes, ex-Fuerzas Especiales, Mexican Special Forces. Two years in a military prison and a dishonourable discharge for putting his commanding officer in hospital.'

Lastly, Howard pulled out a grainy CCTV still photo of a thin-faced, lean man and handed it to Danny.

'Andre Kristoff, ex-Spetsnaz, Russian Special Forces. Other than that, we know little about him.'

Danny sat looking at the pictures of the men for a long time, his features hard, his eyes cold, unreadable. The tension in the room grew in uneasy silence until he finally spoke.

'What's my way in?'

CHAPTER 10

After driving for hours, Gregor turned off the main road and headed down the winding dirt track high in the hills that lay 40km outside of Novi Pazar, Serbia. The truck bounced and rocked along the rock-covered, potholed track. Eventually the trees thinned to a clearing around a large, traditional Serbian farmhouse and its outbuildings. Nikolai Korentski stepped out of the front door. He brushed his shoulder-length, dark wavy hair back out of his eyes, straightened his expensive leather jacket over his Armani shirt and turned excitedly to his brother Ivan.

'Ha, you see, brother. All your worrying is for nothing,' he said, throwing his arms in the air as Gregor and Bosko approached in the truck.

Ivan remained silent. He didn't share his brother's enthusiasm. A hard time in the Russian army and a harder time in Moscow's notorious Butyrka jail had left him naturally pessimistic. Even though he was only a couple of years older than Nikolai, he looked more like ten. His face was lined, and his salt and pepper cropped hair was trenched with tram-lined scar tissue working its way down through his left ear. It was during that knife attack in Butyrka jail that Gregor had saved him by breaking a porcelain sink in half with his attacker's head.

'Hey, Gregor, open up the back, let me see the merchandise,' said Nikolai, slapping Gregor on the back as he walked to the rear of the truck.

Towering over Nikolai, Gregor lowered the lift and opened the back. They climbed in and waited for Ivan, who appeared at the lift with a large crowbar.

'Hey, Nikki, you are going to need this,' said Ivan, climbing up to join them.

'*Da*, thank you, brother. Open it, Gregor.'

Grabbing the crowbar, Gregor jammed it under the crate lid and popped it open in one swift movement. His face beaming, Nikolai picked up one of the Pentic rifles. He grabbed one of the loaded magazines and turned to leave the truck.

'Look at this, hey. Come grab one. Let's see what these fuckers can do,' he said jumping down to the ground on the passenger side of the truck next to Bosko.

They followed him round the side of the farmhouse. He pointed at an old rusty tractor growing into the meadow fifty metres away. Lining up, they clicked the rifles to automatic and fired. Even with suppressors, the rifles echoed around the valley. They burned through the 30-round magazines in a fraction of a second. The high velocity tungsten carbide rounds ripped through the old tractor. The powerful impact rocked it in the overgrown grass, the bullets shattering the engine block.

'Woohoo, fucking A!' yelled Nikolai, walking over to take a closer look at the tractor.

'The English really came good, da,' said Gregor to Ivan.

'Mmm,' said Ivan, frowning.

'What's the matter, Ivan, you don't trust them?'

'I don't trust anyone, Gregor, especially that fucking fanatical lunatic Belhadj,' said Ivan, handing him the rifle.

'Has he not agreed to pay for the rifles, brother?'

'Yes. When we get to the port. But I'm not happy. This English guy gives us rifles and body armour for nothing. All we have to do to get the money is sell them to a Libyan terrorist,' said Ivan, looking over at his excited brother by the tractor.

'Nikolai doesn't seem worried,' said Gregor, looking in Nikolai's direction.

'Nikolai is never worried. He just sees the money, that's why I have to look after him.'

'Relax, Ivan. We do the deal and split the money. Easy,' said Gregor trying to lift Ivan's mood.

'When Belhadj uses stolen British weapons to over-throw, seize power and kill his prime minister, questions will be asked.'

'And we will be long gone, Ivan. When do we take the guns to the boat?' said Gregor.

'Hmm, I hope so. The container ship will be at Durrës on Friday, Nikolai and Bosko will drive down Thursday and stay the night.'

'*Da*, is good,' said Gregor as Bosko and Nikolai caught up.

'Now we drink. Celebrate!' shouted Nikolai storming off in front towards the farmhouse.

CHAPTER 11

Two days after his meeting, Edward pulled up outside Danny's house. The front door opened before he knocked so he walked in to see Danny disappearing into the kitchen.

'We all set?' Danny asked, draining a mug of tea and placing it in the dishwasher.

'Yep, my guy says Benton's back at his house.'

'Considering the fate of my predecessor, how do I know I can trust your guy?' said Danny with a look not to be argued with.

'I thought you'd be worried about that, so I've drafted in Thomas Trent and John Ball. You know them both and they've been abroad for the last six months providing security support to UN workers, so there's no link to the department,' said Edward, happy to see Danny's face relax a little.

Danny had worked with and trusted both men. A few years ago they stopped a terrorist cell led by Marcus Tenby from executing a cyber-attack of monumental proportions on America's financial institutions. He'd worked with Tom again to stop a group called The Board and their paid assassin known as the Chinaman.

'Ok, good. Let's go.'

Edward took the A406 on the hour-long journey in heavy traffic across London to the suburb of Hounslow.

'So what's the plan?' said Danny, glancing absentmindedly at the traffic.

'Howard's sorted two top floor flats that overlook Benton's house. Tom and John are keeping surveillance from one and you're staying next door in the other. Your cover story is you're down on your luck and skint, the council housed you in the flat a month ago.'

'Ok, so how do I find a way in?' said Danny turning to face Edward.

'Rex Benton and his friends are keeping a low profile since Tripp's death. He takes a daily walk, goes shopping and then goes home again. Every few days they all meet at a pub, The Moon Under Water, a few hundred metres from the flat. Tom's come up with a plan to get you notice when they're all in there,' said Edward, turning off to drive through Brentford.

'Ok, say I get in, which seems like a pretty fucking big if. What's my modus operandi?'

'Get in and find out what they're planning, find out who's behind this and who the buyer is.'

'Thank fuck for that, for a moment I thought you were going to give me something difficult to do,' said Danny managing a smile.

Edward pulled the car over unexpectedly and looked at Danny with an intense stare. 'Are you sure you're up for this, Danny?'

'I owe Howard,' Danny said without looking at him.

'That's not what I asked.'

'I served with Rex Benton on several missions, he even saved my life on one of them. He was a bloody good soldier,' Danny replied, turning to look Edward in the eye.

'Will that compromise your mission?' Edward said after a pause.

'No,' was all Danny said in reply, the look on his face plainly saying the conversation was over.

They drove in silence for the rest of the trip. Edward had known Danny long enough to know when he was best left alone. Finally entering Hounslow, Edward turned up Staines Road. He pointed out the pub as they drove past, before turning right into Cromwell Road. They entered a car park next to a 1960s ten-storey block of flats set in the middle of two-storey blocks of council houses.

'Home sweet home,' said Danny, grabbing his old army kitbag off the back seat.

Edward tapped a door entry fob against the pad by the foyer door. The lock buzzed, allowing them to pull the door and enter. Pressing the button for the lift, he noticed Danny looking to the stairs.

'It's the top floor,' he said, already knowing Danny's answer.

'I'll meet you up there,' said Danny, handing his bag over before heading up the stairs, leaping up them two at a time. A habit left over from his service days, Danny still had an aversion to being in a confined space with only one exit. No cover, no defence; the perfect kill box. He hit the top floor landing only thirty seconds behind Edward. His pulse had quickened, but he was far from out of breath.

'Right, that's your flat,' said Edward, pointing to the next door down the landing as he knocked on the one in front of him.

The door opened and Tom's smiling face looked out at them.

'Morning, boss,' he said to Edward.

'Tom,' Edward said, giving a small nod as he walked in.

'Danny, it's good to see you, man,' he said as the two gave each other a quick embrace and slap on the back.

'I'm glad you've got my back, mate,' Danny said giving Tom a knowing look that only two men who'd seen action together would get. 'John, good to see you again, it's been a while,' Danny said as he moved into the living room.

'Yeah, it's taken me this long to get over it,' John said with a chuckle as he shook Danny's hand firmly.

'I'll agree with that. What have we got here then?' Danny said stepping over to the long-lensed cameras on tripods by the window and a table with computer screens and laptops set up with pictures and camera feeds.

'Take a look,' John said, pointing to one of the screens.

'Rex Benton's house?' Danny said, taking his eyes off the heavily magnified picture of a house to squint out the window, trying to pick it out on the street.

'Yep, he went out on foot about half an hour ago. These two are traffic cam feeds from the corner of Cromwell Road and another on Staines Road by The Moon Under Water pub,' John said, pointing them out.

'Over here we've got five hidden camera feeds with full audio from the flat next door, so no hookers or sheep shagging, ok?' grinned Tom tapping the screen.

'Can you bug his house or get surveillance on the street?'

'Not a chance, this guy's a machine. He's like a bloody predator, top of the food chain, sixth sense or something. He reminds me a lot of you. We've tried to get close with vans for surveillance; he's at the window staring straight at us before we've got within a hundred metres of the place. As for the house, it's Fort fucking Knox, alarmed to the hilt and dead-bolted windows and doors,' said Tom sitting down at the table.

'So, Tom, what's this plan to get me into this group?' Danny said, taking a seat next to him.

CHAPTER 12

Leaving his house, Rex Benton walked a well-rehearsed route. It took him down to the main road towards the shops. His eyes never stopped moving, constantly checking parked vehicles, passing cars and reflections in shop windows for telltale signs of being following. Satisfied, he cut through a housing estate and took a walkway that emerged only two roads over from his house. As a final precaution, he walked to the end of the road, then doubled back to a plain-looking Ford Escort. He climbed in and drove off, driving cautiously, keeping to the speed limit. The stolen car had new registration plates, copied from an identical car belonging to a doctor who lived a few miles away. The plates would never flag on any traffic cameras or patrol cars as a vehicle of interest. Even so, Benton took a route round the back streets, checking his mirrors for tails before turning back to the main road and heading out of London.

Forty minutes later he pulled off the A3 at Guildford and turned into a large retail park. He moved to the far side of the car park with no CCTV coverage previously checked out by Kristoff. Reversing into a parking place next to a red Audi A4, he came side by side with Miguel Mendes in the passenger seat. They exchanged a curt nod before Rex got out, locked the Escort and got in the back of the Audi. The second the door shut, Peter Knowles pulled away, driving steadily out of the car park.

'Right, final check before we get there. No one's got a mobile on them?' said Benton bluntly.

'No, boss,' they said in unison.

'Where did you get the car from?' Benton questioned.

'Stolen, boss, family's away on holiday. The car won't be missed for a fortnight. And yes, I've removed the GPS unit,' said Knowles, giving a wink in the rear-view mirror.

'Good man, we don't want anything that could be used in the future to put us in this location,' said Benton, pulling some plans out of his jacket pocket.

They drove out of Guildford, turning along a small country lane, before heading down a farm track and finally parking under the cover of trees. Bailing out of the car, they headed through the woods, instinctively spreading out and walking in formation, keeping their eyes and ears open. They'd covered nearly a mile when Benton's hand went up. Even in civvies, the team melted away silently behind the trees. Up ahead, a dog walker wandered down the track. His springer spaniel stopped and stared into the trees for a few seconds. A call from his master's voice broke his curiosity and he turned and bounded after him excitedly. As soon as he was out of sight, the team slid back into view and continued on their journey. They made their way up an incline, tucking behind a low hedge by the edge of the woods.

'Kristoff,' said Benton, sticking his arm out.

Sliding the rucksack off his back, Kristoff pulled a large pair of field binoculars out and handed them to Benton. He looked through them while Kristoff pulled out the scope from his sniper rifle and checked out the view.

Half a mile away, tucked in the dip below them, lay Centrex research centre, its collection of large industrial buildings surrounded by two fifteen-foot razor-wire-topped fences.

'Kristoff, you see the guardhouse left of the gate?' Benton said.

'*Da*, is big. How many guards?' said Kristoff, passing the scope to Mendes.

'Intel says six in the house, two on the gate and four patrolling the estate. They rotate on six-hour shifts, day and night.'

'Armed?' said Knowles.

'Yep, government CPNI men with standard issue Glock 17 handguns and MP5 rifles,' said Benton handing Knowles the binoculars.

'Which door do we use for access to the package?' said Knowles, scanning the facility.

'Past the guardhouse, the blue unit on the left, red loading door. We'll have to go in the door on the far corner to open it from the inside.'

'Where are the alarms and CCTV control panels, boss?' said Mendes looking at Benton.

'There's a comms room in the guardhouse.'

'If we get the go ahead, we definitely need a fifth man. Mendes and one other to take out the guardhouse and comms, Kristoff to bring the truck in, while me and you take out stray guards and get the package to the loading bay,' said Knowles, handing the binoculars back to Benton.

'Yes, we do. Until then, we plan and rehearse. Our employer will supply passes to get us through the gate. I expect fifteen minutes gate to gate,' said Benton, folding the plans and moving back into the trees.

The other three all looked at each other. They knew better than to ask Benton who their employer was. Finally, Mendes shrugged and turned after him, closely followed by the others.

CHAPTER 13

After a six-hour drive and an uneventful border crossing from Serbia to Albania, Nikolai and Bosko arrived in the port town of Durrës. They stopped in a hotel for the night. High on the anticipation of a large payout, the two of them ate and drank heavily before turning in.

'Come on, move your arse, Bosko, let's get this done,' said Nikolai climbing into the passenger side of the truck.

'Ok, ok, I'm coming,' said Bosko wandering around the cab rubbing his head.

'What's the matter, can't keep up, old man?' Nikolai laughed as Bosko got in the driver's seat.

'I think you poisoned me with that fucking Albanian raki. My head feels like it's been hit with a shovel,' Bosko said, starting the lorry up.

'Don't worry. You'll feel better when you see all that money.'

The hotel was close to the port and in less than five minutes the truck pulled up to the port authority's gate. Nikolai wound down the window and handed over the fake consignment paperwork supplied by Hamish in London. Unimpressed and only half-awake in his early morning shift, the port official flicked through the paperwork without close inspection. Nikolai's heart pounded when the official's forehead creased as he hovered over the last page. Nikolai breathed a sigh of relief when he put them down and thumped his rubber stamp of approval on each sheet.

'The MSC Carmen is on the far side, bay 18,' the port official said, handing the paperwork back to Nikolai.

Not trusting his voice, Nikolai just nodded and gestured Bosko to drive on.

'Fuck, he almost gave me a heart attack,' said Nikolai grinning and breathing heavily.

'What's the matter, can't hold your nerve, boy?' said Bosko grinning, returning Nikolai's earlier dig.

'Ok, ok, very funny. Go round to the left.'

The huge container ship moored at the far end was clearly visible. Two large cranes worked the front and back, carefully lifting and stacking containers from the quay onto the decks. When they got close, a black African and an Arabic-looking man stepped out from behind a container. They swung the AK-47s hanging from their sides up and indicated for Bosko to drive into one of the storage ware-houses running parallel to the quayside.

'Here we go,' said Bosko driving in through the loading doors, the shady gloom inside making it hard to see until their eyes accustomed from the bright sunlight outside.

Bosko pulled to a halt in front of four more armed men in robes and headdresses that covered their faces leaving only cold, hard eyes visible through the slits.

The two at either end moved forward and yelled. 'Out!'

'Ok, easy,' said Nikolai climbing down from the cab.

Ushered to the front of the truck by men jabbing the AKs at them, their hearts raced and eyes went wide when the two men in front pulled the slides back on their guns and brought them up to the shoulder.

'Wait, what, fuck, no no no!' shouted Nikolai, pushing himself back into the truck, waving his hands at the men.

A loud yell from behind them caused the men to step back and stand to attention. A short, round, Arabic man walked through the gap and extended his hand.

'You must be Nikolai, I am Abdel Belhadj,' he said, shaking their hands vigorously. 'I am sorry for your reception, but one cannot be too careful.'

'Yes, of course,' Nikolai said, still shaking.

'Please, may we see the merchandise?' said Belhadj, moving to the rear of the truck.

Bosko opened the back and lifted the lid off one of the wooden crates. He pulled out one of the Pentics and handed it to Belhadj. Taking it, Belhadj's eyes gleamed as he turned it over in front of him.

'Very good, my friend, you have been invaluable to the cause,' he said waving to a man on a forklift.

His man drove in and skillfully lifted the crates out of the truck. Belhadj shouted to someone else who scooted in nervously carrying a large silver case. He placed it on the back of the truck and flicked the catches, opening the lid to show the contents. Nikolai's grin returned as the bundles of $100 bills came into view.

'It's been a pleasure dealing with you, but now I must bid you farewell. I have a plane to catch,' said Belhadj, shaking their hands one last time before wandering off to a waiting car. The armed men moved out of the warehouse following the forklift as it moved the crate into a container outside. After watching them go, Nikolai and Bosko turned to look at each other.

'Let's get the fuck out of here,' said Nikolai, slamming the case shut with a grin. Bosko didn't need telling twice.

He shut the back of the truck and hastily got in the driver's seat. Crunching the truck into reverse, Bosko drove them out of the warehouse. Behind them one of the large cranes picked up the container of guns, taking it high in the air and swinging it towards the container ship. Bosko and Nikolai left the port, driving through the industrial area on their way to the main road out of Durrës.

'How about that, Bosko? We get back and celebrate tonight, my friend. I nearly fucking shit myself when they pointed their guns at us,' said Nikolai, getting his phone out.

'By the smell in this cab I thought you had,' laughed Bosko.

Nikolai laughed back and dialled his brother. 'Hey, Ivan, your little brother's done the deal. We're on our way back.'

A big white Nissan patrol pulled sharply in front of them as Nikolai talked.

'Hey, fucking Albanian drivers,' shouted Bosko, throwing hand gestures out the window. The 4x4 jammed on the brakes in front. As Bosko did the same, he noticed a van driving up tight behind them, boxing them in.

'I don't fucking like this, Nikki.'

'Hang on, Ivan. What the fuck is this clown playing at?' said Nikolai to Bosko.

At that point the doors swung open and the three passengers got out, fast. Western-looking men with military style haircuts, shades and dark jackets, each one brandishing a Pentic carbine rifle. Staring at Nikolai with his rifle pointing up at Nikolai's head, the middle man stepped forward.

'The general sends his regards,' he said, tensing to fire.

'Oh god, no. Ivan, the gen—' they cut Nikolai short with a hail of armour-piercing rounds ripping through the cab of the truck. Its thin metal and glass offering no protection as the bullets tore Nikolai and Bosko's bodies into a bloody pulp before exiting through the back of the cab and out through the roof of the truck.

The man in the middle raised his hand, stopping the fire immediately. While the outer two looked round to cover the perimeter, he opened the cab door, reached in and took the blood-covered case of money. Noticing Nikolai's phone still displaying the live call to Ivan, he picked it up.

He could hear Ivan shouting, 'Nikki, Nikki!' When Ivan went silent, he put it to his ear.

'Bang, you're dead,' he said, hanging up and throwing it back into the cab.

He walked to the front spinning his finger in the air, signalling it was time to move. The passengers were in the car and gone within seconds, closely followed by the van from behind.

CHAPTER 14

'What is it Nikki? Who's there with you?' Ivan shouted down the phone. When he got no reply he pressed the phone firmly into his ear, straining to hear.

He heard, 'The general sends his regards,' spoken faintly in the background.

'Oh god, no. Ivan, the gen—' came Nikolai's panicked voice echoing down the phone before being cut short by a deafening hail of metallic pings and shattering glass.

'Nikki, Nikki!' Ivan shouted, his face pale and his hand trembling.

'Bang, you're dead,' came a cold, confident voice before the phone cut off.

'What's wrong, Ivan?' asked Gregor, watching Ivan's shocked face as he slowly lowered the phone.

'Ivan!' Gregor shouted, trying to snap him out of it.

The gravity of what had just happened hit Ivan like a bolt of lightning.

'Nikki is dead. We've been screwed over, Gregor. We must go. Now, right now!' he shouted, running to the table.

Picking up a Pentic, Ivan hurriedly loaded it. Gregor grabbed one of the others, following Ivan's lead. As they put spare mags in their pockets and loaded the handguns, a large 4x4 passed across the CCTV camera feed covering the dirt track to the farmhouse.

'Fuck, let's go, now. Out the back, quick. We'll swing round through the trees,' Ivan said, his voice hushed as if the intruders could hear him.

The pair flew out of the back door, sprinting the thirty metres across the meadow to the tree line. Once behind cover, Gregor indicated he'd circle round behind the wood sheds, while Ivan worked his way through the trees. Knowing the woods like the backs of their hands, Gregor and Ivan moved out of sight, circling around until Gregor was above the track watching four men dressed in dark combat gear edging their way towards the farmhouse, their automatic weapons poised.

Ivan crept his way further back until he was only ten feet away from the intruders' 4x4. The driver was out of the vehicle standing with his back to Ivan, watching his four team members as they approached the farmhouse. Ivan slid a large hunting knife from its sheath on his belt. Emerging from the bushes, he trod lightly up behind the driver. In one swift movement Ivan put his hand around and clamped it over the driver's mouth, thrusting the knife in and up into the base of his skull. The man rag-dolled, flopping to the ground, long dead before he hit it. Putting the knife back in its sheath, Ivan raised the Pentic rifle and made his way along the track back to the farmhouse. Instinctively knowing where Gregor would be, he signalled for him to follow down with him.

The two of them turned the last corner in the track. Ahead of them, four gunmen faced away, slowly approaching the farmhouse beyond. Gregor and Ivan looked at each other and gave a nod, turning back to the gunmen they unloaded the rifles. The armour-piercing rounds ripped them into pieces. Blood and masonry flew around in a cloud of dusty red. The chaos lasted only a few seconds before an eerie silence replaced it. As they walked closer, they could see one man still moving, his eyes wide and scared, blood oozing from bullet holes in his chest and stomach. Ivan stood over him.

'Who is the general, huh?' he said, pressing his boot on the man's stomach.

'Argh, fuck off.'

Barely waiting for his words to leave his mouth, Ivan put a bullet through the man's kneecap.

'The general, who is he?' he said over the man's screams.

'Please no, he's General—Rufus—Rufus McManus,' the man answered, breathing heavily through gritted teeth.

Ivan drew his handgun without visible emotion, put three bullets in the man's head, then stood there motionless, the smoking gun still pointed at the man. It took a few long seconds before he spoke.

'Get the digger out of the shed, Gregor. We bury these bastards in case anyone comes looking. Then we go to London and avenge Nikki and Bosko's deaths.'

'Yes, Ivan. I will call Karl and let him know we are coming.'

'Thank you, my friend,' said Ivan, finally lowering the gun as he looked tearfully at Gregor.

Ivan searched all the bodies and the 4x4, but the gunmen were pros—no papers, no ID. The only things he found were two burner phones with no contacts, and three white hotel key cards with no name.

An hour later there were five people buried under the meadow with a big pile of manure placed on top to disguise the freshly dug soil. After a last look around, Ivan pulled the farmhouse door shut and followed Gregor to the 4x4. Squeezing his large frame behind the wheel, Gregor spun the vehicle round and headed up the dirt track towards the main road.

CHAPTER 15

General Rufus McManus smiled to himself as he entered the meeting room in the Home Office before anyone else had arrived. He moved round the table and purposefully took the seat at the top. With his folder on the desk he sat confidently staring across the room, waiting for the others to arrive. The Prime Minister came in next, with the Minister for Defence, William Pringle, predictably kissing his arse close behind. Rufus watched Pringle with great satisfaction, noting his annoyance at Rufus's early arrival. They waited patiently until Alfred Burrows, the Deputy Prime Minister, and Howard arrived to take their seats.

'Right. Good afternoon, gentlemen. As we're all here, shall we begin? General, I believe you have some news for us?'

'Yes, thank you, Prime Minister. I am pleased to say that earlier this morning Project Dragonfly tracked the Serbian criminal unit responsible for the recent theft of the MoD equipment. We caught up with them just after the rifles and body armour had been sold to a terrorist named

Abdel Belhadj, and loaded onto a container vessel in Durrës, Albania. The Royal Navy intercepted the vessel bound for Libya, and the weapons are safely back in our possession,' said Rufus, playing his trump card to the table with great satisfaction.

'That is indeed good news, General, and we thank you for your tireless determination in getting this matter resolved. However, the Minister for Defence has presented the Security Council with a compelling argument for Howard's special division of the Secret Intelligence Services to absorb the role of Project Dragonfly under its existing budget,' said the Prime Minister while Pringle nodded and stared triumphantly across the table at Rufus.

'With all due respect, Mr Pringle has not got a clue what the security of this country requires. I respect Howard and the intelligence services, but there are threats that require the very specific skills that Project Dragonfly offers. To terminate the project at this time would be a grave mistake and one that will come at a high price,' said Rufus, his face flushed in anger.

'I'm sorry, General, this government cannot continue to justify the multi-million-pound appropriation of taxpayers' money to keep Project Dragonfly operational. Our own intelligence services do an incredible job of keeping our country safe. Project Dragonfly can continue to run while we re-shuffle Howard's special division, at which time I will shelve the project,' the Prime Minister said, closing his file to indicate the end of the meeting.

Rufus stood and left, ignoring Pringle who held out his hand with a smug look on his face. Leaving the building, he marched his way towards his office. Taking care not to be followed, Rufus took a different route than usual, taking him past an independent phone shop. He went in and paid cash as before for a cheap pay-as-you-go phone. Ripping the packaging off, he powered it up and dialled the number from memory.

'Yes.'

'Pringle's still trying to shut us down. I don't care how you do it, find a replacement for Tripp and get the job done. I have Abdel Belhadj's brother, Jarrel's hair and fingerprint samples to plant once you've dispensed with your little bunch of renegades. Get it done, Rex, I need you back in Dragonfly,' said Rufus, hanging up without waiting for an answer. He took a handkerchief out of his pocket, rubbed the phone clean and dumped it casually in the nearest bin. Still angry, Rufus continued on his journey, lost in his own thoughts.

Goddamn modern age, politically correct, peace-loving pricks. It looks like I'll have to dispose of Howard along with Pringle and the PM.

Across the city in Hounslow, Benton stopped walking. Lowering the phone, he snapped it in half and slid it into the nearest bin. Pulling a new phone out of his jacket pocket, he turned it on. As soon as it got a signal, he dialled a number from memory. Tapping in a code at the prompt, he set the phone as the new divert, then hung up. His contact number was a virtual phone located in Germany. It diverted through two more virtual phones before forwarding to Benton's latest burner phone. Tucking it into his pocket, he walked down and entered an underpass as two men came towards him. They were young, fit, and had the look of regular gym-goers. Benton wasn't particularly interested in them until one barged his shoulder, refusing to step to one side so they could both pass.

'Oi, fucking look where you're going. Fucking idiot,' he

said out loud, more in a testosterone display of machoism to his buddy than as a direct challenge to Benton.

Without saying a thing, Benton stopped stock still with his back to them, unnoticed, as they walked away. His eye twitched and a cloud of rage filled his head. The men strutted side by side along the hedge-lined path leading from the underpass. Neither of them saw Benton until he stamped on the back of the knee of the one who'd barged him. As the man fell backwards, Benton chopped him hard in the throat, sending him slamming to the floor choking.

His buddy's reactions were fast. He danced on his toes with his fists up, obviously a boxer of sorts. Benton eyes were wild and glassy. He breezed inside the other's defence and exploded in a blistering display of mixed martial arts: blow after blow to the body, followed by a knee to the groin. With the wind knocked out of the man, he doubled-up in pain. Folding his arm up to launch the hard bone of his elbow, Benton focused the kinetic energy of his moving body into one spot, striking the man like the blow from a hammer under his chin. The result was explosive. The man shot back upright before flipping off his feet onto his back, out cold.

Reality flashed and twisted in Benton's mind. He could see, hear and smell the rancid, piss-smelling room the ISIS soldiers beat and tortured him in for three months. Reliving the moment he killed his capturers and escaped, Benton leaped onto the choking man's chest and rained brutal punches to his face.

'Bastards! Fucking bastard!' he yelled as he shattered the man's jaw and flattened his nose.

As quickly as it started, it stopped. The present suddenly blew the images away, leaving him staring at the unconscious man lying under his blood-covered knuckles. Keen and alert once more, he checked his surroundings for observers. Seeing none, he wiped the blood off his hands onto the man's shirt, got up and hurried through the underpass.

Calm and controlled once more, he turned onto Staines Road and continued towards the town centre, checking for followers as he went. He walked past The Moon Under Water pub and checked the reflection in a shop door opposite before turning back and entering the pub.

CHAPTER 16

U p on the tenth floor in the surveillance flat, John spun the chair away from the traffic cam monitors.

'Get golden bollocks next door to shake a leg. Benton's just entered the pub to meet the others.'

'On it,' said Tom, leaping off the sofa and dashing to the neighbouring flat.

He didn't get a chance for the second knock: the door flew inwards, and Danny gave Tom a grin as he walked past him, tense and alert with pre-mission excitement.

'You ready for this, Tom?' he asked over his shoulder.

'Ready as I'll ever be,' Tom replied, opening the door to the surveillance flat. 'Everything still good, John?'

'Yep, all four of them are in there.'

Danny turned to the two of them as they headed down the stairs. 'Remember, no holding back. They'd spot a fake a mile off, ok?'

Both men nodded, as they continued out of the building.

———

Entering the pub, Danny went straight to the bar without looking round. He knew Benton and his guys would sit in the corner booth with its view of the entrance and bar one way, and view through the dining area to the back door and pub garden the other. It's where he would have sat. The hairs on the back of his neck stood up and he could feel Benton's eyes boring into him as recognition hit home. He ordered a pint and remained at the bar, pretending to look at his phone. Half of his pint later two guys entered the pub and stood either side of Danny, their faces hard and chests puffed out in their black bomber jackets.

Here we go, lights, camera, action.

'Oi, Pearson. Mr Ball wants his money back. No excuses,' the taller guy said, leaning in menacingly.

Danny sipped his pint slowly before placing it down on the bar. 'Listen, twinkle toes, tell Mr Ball to fuck off and find my ex. Ask her for it, it's her debt.'

'We're not fucking about. Money. NOW!' he said, placing a hand on Danny's shoulder.

Danny turned his head slowly as he slipped off the bar stool and tuned to face them.

'Ok, ok, not here. Out the back in the pub garden,' he said, cocking his head towards the rear door.

As he walked through the pub, he caught eye contact with Benton for the first time. Danny gave a small nod of acknowledgement and received the same from Benton as he walked past. Pushing the door to the pub garden wide so it stayed open, allowing a clear view from Benton's seat. Danny waited until the two men following closed in, he spun and landed a blisteringly fast combination of punches to the tall guy's body then an uppercut under his chin. He went down in a daze, but his short stocky partner was quick and caught Danny with a powerful punch to the side of his face. Knocked sideways, Danny twisted and caught the man off guard as he kicked him in the balls with all his might. The guy's face went purple as he doubled-up. Danny kneed him in the face as he bent forward, instantly knocking him back upright, then over onto his back. Turning back to the tall guy to finish him, Danny stopped when he held up his hand in surrender.

'Alright, leave it, we're going,' he gasped, struggling to get to his feet.

'Get your mate and fuck off. I don't want to see you again. Got it?' Danny said, picking the stocky guy up and pushing him towards his partner.

The two of them held each other up and staggered away through the pub garden. Danny brushed himself off and walked casually back through the pub. He sat back down on his stool, drained his pint and waved it at the barman for a top up.

'Hello, Rex,' Danny said without turning round.

'Daniel Pearson, you always did have eyes in the back of your head,' came the distinctive voice of Commander Rex Benton from behind him.

Danny turned. The two of them stared at each other intensely for a few seconds. As if on cue they both broke into a grin and hugged, patting each other on the back.

'Fuck, Rex. Good to see you, man,' Danny said, genuinely meaning it despite his mission.

'You too, mate. What was all that with Laurel and Hardy?'

'Oh, nothing. Bloody ex had a habit of spending too much and borrowing off the wrong people, hence the Chuckle Brothers,' said Danny looking over at Benton's table with three mean and moody military types staring back at him.

'What the fuck's that, ex-soldiers anonymous?' he said nodding their way.

'Ha, yeah, something like that. Come over and have a pint, I'll introduce you,' said Benton with a grin.

'Nah, I wouldn't want to interrupt date night,' Danny smirked.

'Fuck off, you twat, grab your drink and join us.'

'Alright, but I'm not sleeping with anyone on the first date,' laughed Danny getting off the stool and following Benton.

'Right, guys, this is Danny Pearson. He's an old Regiment mate of mine so make him welcome,' said Benton shooting them a warning look that didn't go unnoticed by Danny.

'Hey, tough guy, sit yourself down here,' said Kristoff, sliding along the seat and nodding for Danny to sit.

———

Several hours and several pints later, Danny climbed the stairs to the top-floor flat. He knocked next door and waited until John swung the door open, holding a bag of frozen peas to his head.

'Just go next door for us, mate, put the light on and show yourself at the window drawing the curtains. Tom's got eyes on from the road,' said John, wincing in pain when he tried to smile.

'Ok mate,' said Danny following the instructions before coming back to the observation flat.

The lounge was in darkness, with Tom looking through the lens of the powerful camera.

'What you got, Tom?'

'Have a look,' said Tom stepping back.

As he looked through the lens, Rex Benton's image

filled it. He stood perfectly still, looking up at Danny's flat with narrowed eyes. Two minutes passed by before he turned slowly and walked towards his house.

'Looks like you've made an impression. How'd it go?' asked Tom, drawing the curtains behind the cameras before he turned a lamp on.

'A lot of barracks banter and mission tales. They're a very tight bunch. Benton's definitely the boss. No talk of what they've been up to as you might expect, but Benton took an interest in what I've been doing for work,' said Danny noticing the red swelling around Tom's eye where he'd hit him earlier.

'You stick to the cover story?'

'Yeah, skint—cleaned out by the ex—and doing the odd bit of contract work at Greenwood Security which will stand up with Paul if they check it out. How's your face?'

'It's fine, lucky for me you punch like a girl,' Tom said, laughing.

'I'm not sure John would agree with you,' said Danny, looking over at John as he sat on the sofa still holding the bag of frozen peas to his head.

'Where there's blame, there's a claim,' said John, forgetting himself again and wincing as he tried to smile for the second time.

'Well, while you two love birds decide who goes on top, I'm off to bed.'

CHAPTER 17

Danny was up early. The sounds of the new flat were playing on his sub-conscious, preventing him from entering deep sleep. He put on his running gear and went out to pound the streets. With his mind cleared and body firing on all cylinders, he returned to the flat and jumped in the shower. Dressed and towel-drying his unruly mop of dark curly hair, he got the sense that something in the flat had changed. The hairs on the back of his neck stood up, and he felt cold chill down his spine. Sliding the wardrobe door open slowly and quietly, he slid his hand inside his old army kit bag and pulled out a razor-sharp commando knife. Padding barefoot across the carpet, Danny moved silently out of the bedroom and along the hall towards the living room. Moving the knife so the blade was between his fingertips, ready to throw, Danny stayed out of sight, listening. He quieted his breathing, letting his senses get in tune with the sounds of the flat.

Nothing. Wait—a sound, a creak of furniture. The sofa.

Zeroing in on the sound, Danny spun into the room with his knife arm raised, ready to throw. Recognition kicked in a split-second before he launched the razor-sharp knife at the figure on the sofa.

'Rex, shit. I nearly fucking killed you. How did you get in?' said Danny, breathing a sigh of relief.

'Easy, a fucking three-year-old could get through that lock. Come on, I'm taking you for breakfast. I've got something I want to talk to you about,' said Benton still sitting on the sofa, totally unfazed by Danny bursting out from the hall with his knife raised.

'Ok, but I'm having the full monty. You scared the shit out of me,' said Danny, dropping the knife on the table and disappearing back to the bedroom to put his shoes and socks on.

'Right, I'm ready, let's go,' Danny said, opening the door for Benton. As he shut it behind him, he gave a wink to one of the hidden cameras for Tom and John next door.

Danny walked with Benton towards Hounslow High Street. Although it was nothing more than a movement of the eyes or a glance at the reflection of a passing car, Danny noticed Benton's discreet checks to see if anyone was following them. They entered a cafe that looked like it hadn't changed since the fifties. Benton headed straight for the back of the room, taking a seat with his back against the wall and a view of the front window and entrance. Danny slid into a seat under the retro red Bakelite table top.

They ordered two mega breakfasts. Danny waited until the waitress moved away before leaning in towards Benton.

'Ok, what's this all about, Rex? You broke into my flat and you checked if we were being followed at least five times on the way here. Now you're sitting there watching the door like you're waiting for war to break out.'

'In our line of work it pays to be careful. You know

that,' said Benton, his light blue-grey eyes solidly fixed on Danny's.

'I don't have a line of work,' Danny replied with a frown.

'Oh yes, you do. It's what they trained you for. I saw the way you took those guys out at the pub, you've still got the edge, the hunger. You can't tell me you don't miss the buzz before a mission and the adrenaline of combat?'

'Maybe I do, but I'm not going to pick up a gun and kill people for money. I may be down on my luck, but I'm not a mercenary,' Danny said sitting back, offended.

'I'm not a mercenary,' Benton said, keeping his voice low.

'Ok, then what the fuck are you, because you're really starting to piss me off now.'

'I'm just a soldier fighting for the safety of his country. There's a job coming up and we need an experienced fifth man who we can trust,' Benton said, pausing as the waitress placed the food on the table.

'What's the job and who's it for?' said Danny between mouthfuls.

'We have to steal something. That's all I can tell you.'

'Will we be armed? Against armed guards?' Danny said, looking up from his food.

'Yes,' Benton answered matter-of-fact.

There was a long silenced pause while Danny ate. Eventually he finished and looked up at Benton and spoke. 'How much?'

'£100,000. Paid when the job's done.'

'Terms of engagement?'

'Only as a last resort.'

Not wanting to come across suspiciously keen, Danny looked in deep thought before answering. 'I need to think about it, Rex.'

'Time's short. I'll be in The Moon Under Water tonight. Let me know your decision,' said Benton, standing and putting his hand out to Danny.

Danny shook it and nodded, then watched him leave. Not wanting to follow too soon behind him, Danny waved to the waitress and ordered another coffee.

CHAPTER 18

Martin Trimley found a quiet corner in the vaulted cellar of Gordon's, the oldest wine bar in London. He looked nervously at his watch, snapping his head up at the sound of approaching footsteps on the flagstone floor. Breathing a sigh of relief he smiled at the handsome young waiter approaching, Trimley's face lit up as he toyed with the young man, asking him to run through the wine list. Smiling, he ordered the recommended white and watched the waiter with leering eyes as he walked towards the bar.

'Careful, Martin, that's what got you into this predicament in the first place,' said Rufus dryly.

Trimley's face dropped like a stone as Rufus slid his jacket off and placed it over the chair next to him and sat down.

'What do you want, Rufus?' said Trimley, his dislike for the general clear to see.

'Now, now, Martin, anyone would think you weren't pleased to see me.'

Trimley was about to answer when the waiter returned with his drink.

'Thank you,' he said, watching the man intently as he took Rufus's order and walked away.

'From what I can recall from the video, I seem to remember you like them considerably younger than that. I dread to think what your wife and children would say if it ever got out,' Rufus said, revelling in his power over Trimley.

'Ok, you've made your point. What is it I can do for you?' said Trimley, his body seeming to shrink and crumble as he resigned to the power Rufus had over him.

'The security of this country is under threat. That silver-spooned idiot William Pringle wants to shut down Project Dragonfly and has the Prime Minister's backing. For the good of the country they must be removed,' Rufus said as calmly as if he were discussing the weather.

'What? Have you gone completely mad?' said Trimley, his eyes darting around, panicking as if the whole bar was listening.

'Calm yourself, Martin, we talked of this,' said Rufus, his voice quiet but assertive, his eyes focused on Trimley, sharp and cold, like a bird of prey.

'You're joking. I didn't think you were seriously going to go through with it,' stammered Trimley, trying to control his nerves.

'Am. I. Known. For. My. Jokes?' said Rufus, leaning in as he spelled it out slowly.

'No, no. Sorry, Rufus.'

'Okay then. We stick to the plan. The Minister for Defence and the PM get taken out by the attack. Your schoolboy chum, Alfred Burrows steps up as Prime Minister and makes you Minister for Defence. Project Dragonfly takes out Abdel Belhadj's brother, Jarrel, as the terrorist responsible, seeking revenge for us foiling the theft of MoD weapons by his brother. You get us full future support from the Cabinet as the UK's main security contractor against extreme terrorist threats.'

Lost for words, Trimley sat sipping his drink with a slightly shaky hand.

'Or you can read about yourself and a certain underage rent boy in tomorrow's gossip papers. Your choice, old boy,' said Rufus, ignoring Trimley's face as it drained of colour, and thanking the waiter for his drink.

'You wouldn't dare. I'd expose you and your plans,' said Trimley sitting up trying to look confident and in charge of the situation.

Rufus didn't answer straight away. He took a sip of his drink, placed it carefully back down on the table and fixed Trimley with a chilling stare. 'You'd be dead before you got ten feet from your house.'

The silence hung in the room like a huge weight over Trimley. Finally Rufus got up and put his jacket on. He smiled at Trimley and turned to leave.

'We'll talk soon, Martin. Send my love to the wife and kids, won't you?' he said as he walked away.

Leaning back into the shadows of the low-lit cellar, Trimley shook while tears of self-pity trickled down his cheek.

CHAPTER 19

The white Air Serbia Airbus A320 with its blue and red tail and back-to-back birds crest touched down on Heathrow Terminal 3's runway. The sight of Gregor's huge frame and snarling face when asked if he had anything to declare triggered a full body search for both him and Ivan. They surprised the officers after they were taken to separate rooms; both of them stripped without a word of complaint or a care who was watching. It was something they'd had to do many times in Butyrka jail, often ending in a beating if the guard took offence to them. This time the experience was fast, polite and civilised. The officers raised their eyebrows at the crude prison tattoos telling tales of violence and murder and gang allegiance. With questions and searches satisfied, the pair moved out into the arrivals hall to be met by Gregor's younger brother, Karl, he was slightly shorter but had a similar physique. The two men embraced like an evil tag team in a WWF match.

'Brother, it is good to see you,' Karl said, releasing

Gregor and embracing Ivan who seemed to disappear into Karl's chest.

'I'm sorry to hear about Nikolai. I want you to know I will do anything in my power to help you avenge your brother's death.'

'Thank you, Karl. It's good to see you,' said Ivan looking around, suspicious of airport security and airport CCTV.

Sensing Ivan's apprehension, Karl gestured for them to follow him. 'Come, come, I have a car waiting. Tonight we drink to Nikolai. Tomorrow we start looking for this general. *Da*.'

Ivan smiled and nodded, while Gregor laughed and slapped his brother on the back. 'Lead the way, little brother, and let us drink.'

———

Danny was getting ready to meet Benton down The Moon Under Water pub, when a knock on the door halted him in his tracks. Spotting the commando knife on the table where he'd thrown it earlier, Danny picked it up and opened the door a crack with the knife just out of sight.

'Afternoon, Daniel, mind if I come in?' said Howard with a jovial smile.

Danny didn't answer; he swung the door open, exposing the knife as he turned and walked away.

'Careful, old chap, you might hurt yourself,' Howard joked dryly as he wandered into the flat.

'Get on with it, Howard, I've got to meet Benton soon.'

'So I hear. Congratulations, sterling work. There has been a development: the missing Pentic rifles and body armour have been recovered. No international incident.

All concerned can breathe a sigh of relief. Case closed,' said Howard, brushing the sofa before taking a seat.

'So why is it I'm sensing a but,' said Danny, picking up the sheath and sliding the knife away.

'Perceptive as always, Daniel. I'm having trouble making the link between our thieves, Mr Benton and friends, a group of Serbian criminals, and a Libyan ISIS terrorist.'

'For fear of stating the obvious, you're supposed to be the intelligent one. Can't you just ask whoever recovered them?' shrugged Danny, checking his watch.

'One would think so, wouldn't one? The gentleman in question runs a privately funded department of our national security and is not known for his sharing nature.'

'So where does that leave me? Do I meet Benton and go deeper down the rabbit hole, or do I bale now the rifles are safe?'

Howard sat quietly for a moment, the creases on his forehead giving away his deep thinking.

'We carry on. Something's not right here. The Serbians didn't have the brains or the organisation to pull this off, and I can't see Benton working for fanatical terrorists. Plus, we need to know what this new job is and who they're doing it for.'

'Ok, we go on. Talking of which, I need to get going,' said Danny grabbing his jacket off the back of a chair.

Howard took this as his cue to leave and stood. He opened the door and paused halfway through. 'Watch yourself, Daniel. Tripp was one of my best.'

Danny gave him a nod of acknowledgement and watched him go. He turned to the hidden camera for next door and raised his eyebrows. 'Showtime,' he said, knowing Tom would be watching and listening in the flat next door.

CHAPTER 20

Walking into the pub, Danny knew Benton and the others would be sitting in the usual place. As he stepped up to the bar, he could feel the gaze of four pairs of eyes like a tangible force pressing on the side of his face. Resisting the urge to turn and look, he ordered a pint and waited for it to be served. Thanking the barmaid, he took a sip before turning and heading towards the corner booth and the tight-knit group.

'Danny,' Benton said bluntly as the others moved round to make a space for him to sit.

'Rex. Lads,' Danny said in return, settling confidently into his seat.

'Well, don't keep us in suspense,' said Knowles.

'I'm in,' said Danny, his face still expressionless.

The table went into an instant tense hush; it held for a few long seconds before they all burst into grins and laughs. Raising their glasses, they slapped Danny on the back. Benton sat calmly back and raised his glass with a nod of acknowledgement.

'Ok, alright, cheers guys. So what's the plan?' Danny

said, enjoying the feeling of comradeship he'd missed since leaving the Regiment.

'Not here, not tonight. We'll talk about that tomorrow. Tonight's for celebrating. Welcome to the team,' said Benton to the cheers of the others. Several hours and several pints later, Danny climbed the last flight of stairs to the top-floor flat. He knocked on the door to the observation flat and went in when Tom answered.

'You smell like a brewery. I take it it went well?' said Tom walking back into the living room.

'Yeah, they have accepted me into the team. Benton's picking me up tomorrow to go through the job,' said Danny yawning.

'Here, I've got something for you,' said Tom, picking up a smartphone off the table and throwing it to Danny.

'I've got a phone, mate,' said Danny, pulling out a cheap push button lump not capable of doing anything other than making a call and a basic text.

'Christ! Scott was right, you are a caveman.'

'What?' Danny said, merrily offended.

'We modified this. It sends us your constant location by GPS and phone mast triangulation. Plus it constantly streams audio and video, even when it's turned off,' Tom said as Danny tucked the phone into his pocket.

Reaching into a rucksack hanging on the dining room chair, Tom pulled out a Beretta APX semi-automatic pistol and offered it to Danny.

'No, Benton would spot it a mile off.'

'Ok, if you're sure. We'll be nearby with a strike team if you need us. Just holler into the phone and we'll come running,' said Tom noticing Danny yawn again.

'Great, thanks, Tom. Now unless you've got a pen that shoots tranquilliser darts or an Aston Martin with rockets, I'm going to bed.'

CHAPTER 21

Not wanting to wake up to Rex Benton sitting in a chair watching him, Danny was up and waiting outside the tower block well before the seven o'clock Benton said he would pick him up.

'You guys receiving me?' he said while looking for approaching cars.

The phone in his inside pocket buzzed its acknowledgment just as Benton walked into view.

'What, we're walking there?'

'A careful man lives to fight another day. Come on,' said Benton, walking past Danny towards Staines Road.

Danny followed as Benton walked the same route he had days before, checking reflections and cars for followers, just as he had before. He cut through a housing estate and took a walkway that emerged two roads over from his house. As they walked past a white Ford Transit van, the side door slid open and Benton pushed Danny inside to the arms of Kristoff and Mendes. The van moved away as Benton slid the side door shut behind him. Before he had time to move, Danny found himself at the wrong end of Kristoff and Mendes's Glock 17 handguns.

'What the fuck is this?' Danny protested, his face hardening as his mind raced.

'Nothing personal, we just have to be sure,' said Kristoff.

Benton moved in and patted Danny down. He lifted his shirt and checked his hair for bugs or tracking devices. Finally he took Danny's phone out and passed it to Knowles in the front, who took it and dropped it into an empty metal ammunition box with the rest of the team's mobiles. He flipped the lid shut, cutting off any trackable signals.

'Let him go, he's good. Like I said, a careful man lives to fight another day,' said Benton breaking into a grin as he slapped Danny on the shoulder.

'Yeah, either of you ever pull a gun on me again and you won't be living to fight anyone,' said Danny shrugging off Kristoff and Mendes.

'Ok, ok. Easy, tough guy,' laughed Kristoff putting his hands up in surrender and backing away.

'Right, you two shut the fuck up. We've got a forty-minute drive until we get to the lockup, so settle down.'

———

'Shit, we just lost him,' said Tom staring at the road map on a tablet. Until a second ago it had contained the red tracking dot from Danny's phone.

'What do you want me to do?' said John from the driving seat of the BMW 4x4.

'Keep going towards Twickenham Cemetery and Chertsey Road,' said Tom scanning the road ahead. 'There, pull over, John.'

The radio of one of the tactical strike team guys burst into life.

'What's up, boss?' came the message from the team in the identical BMW following them.

'Sit tight. We've lost signal, over,' said the team leader in the back.

In the front, Tom pulled up the last few minutes of audio before Danny's phone signal disappeared.

'What the fuck is this?' came Danny's slightly muffled voice.

'Nothing personal, we just have to be sure,' came a voice seconds before the audio cut off.

'Whose voice was that?' said Tom.

'The Russian, Kristoff. What was that noise before Danny spoke? Rewind it,' said John, leaning across to hear better.

There was a deep whooshing sound followed by a clunk.

'Car door?'

'No, a sliding door. The side door of a van. They pulled him into a van,' said Tom, pulling out his phone and making a call.

'Thomas, what can I do for you?' came Howard's voice.

'We lost him. They pulled him into a vehicle and searched him. Then the signal died. There's a traffic camera at the junction of Hospital Bridge Road and Percy Road, next to Twickenham Cemetery. I need the feed from 7.20 to 7.40. We're looking for any vans heading for the A316 Chertsey Road. Reg and descriptions. Try to track where they go via traffic cams,' said Tom anxiously checking his watch.

'Do you think his cover's blown?'

'Hard to say, from the audio I'd say it's 50/50.'

'Mmm. Sit tight, I'll get back to you,' said Howard, hanging up without waiting for an answer.

'Shit!' shouted Tom, punching the dash in front of him.

'What now?' said John.

'We wait.'

CHAPTER 22

I t was hard to tell where they were going from the back of the van. Sitting low down his view through the front window only gave him sky, and the occasional tall buildings to the side. They were heading out of London. By the increased roar of jet engines straining to lift impossible tons of metal and bodies into the air, they had passed Heathrow. The sun swung into view, then out of view as the van moved between south and west. They were taking back roads, presumably to avoid the ever-growing sea of cameras lining the motorways. His best guess was they were outside the M25, somewhere in the countryside around Guildford. Eventually the van turned down a dirt track, bumping and rocking for a further quarter of a mile before coming to a halt.

'Tuck the van behind the barn,' said Benton, sliding the side door open.

'Yes boss,' replied Knowles, driving it away as soon as the doors shut.

The place was remote, Danny had to give Benton that. He was standing in front of an old red brick farmhouse, a little run down and tired but still worth a fortune in this neck of the woods. To the side were some low-lying outbuildings and a large barn. Benton and the others headed towards it, waiting at the high double doors while Benton unlocked the large padlock securing them. The barn had a Tardis feel about it, appearing larger on the inside than out. A 7.5-tonne G4S security lorry sat parked just inside. In the large space beside it, the team had set up rows of fold-up camping tables, their surfaces covered with neatly laid out G4S uniforms, Pentic rifles and ammunition, body armour, and black-painted helmets with shaded face masks. Further back the tables were covered with plans, maps and photographs.

'Right, listen up. You three, check and prep everything: radios, the truck, and weapons, strip and clean,' shouted Benton over Knowles and Kristoff's squaddie banter.

'Aw, come on, boss, we've done it a thousand times,' grumbled Mendes.

'And you'll do it a thousand and one times. Now MOVE!' Benton ordered loudly, his face like thunder.

'Yes boss,' said Mendes getting to work sheepishly.

'Danny, over here,' Benton said, turning to the plans.

Moving up beside him, Danny got his first look at the plans of the Centrex research facility. He picked the surveillance pictures up off the table beside them and rifled through the images of the gate and guardhouse and armed guards changing shifts.

'How many guards?' he finally said to Benton.

'Twelve, four on patrol, two on the gate. They rotate with the other six every four hours. A fresh team of CPNI guards come in every three days to relieve them.'

'Mmm, where's the target item?'

'This building here,' said Benton, watching Danny

closely, his focus and mannerisms transporting him back to their SAS days.

'Ok, what's the plan? I'm guessing it involves that lorry and those uniforms,' said Danny pointing in their direction.

'Our client's influence runs far and wide. The research facility receives regular scheduled deliveries from a manufacturing plant in Newcastle. That truck and the fake identities for you, Kristoff and Mendes are on the facilities schedule. You'll be let through the gate and told to park by the guardhouse in this bay here,' Benton said, pointing to the bays on the plan. 'All visitors and deliveries have to be escorted on site, so they'll put you there until they've arranged an escort. Me and Knowles will exit the back of the truck and secure the two guards at gate security. You and Mendes will secure the guardhouse and keep watch. Mendes will take out CCTV, radio and security systems in the comms room located inside. While you're doing that, we will enter the target building and get the object to a loading bay here, where Kristoff will have the truck waiting. We load up and drive out, picking you and Mendes up as we pass,' said Benton, pointing out the buildings and route on the plans as he spoke.

'What about the guards around the site?'

'There's a team of four that patrol the perimeter. As long as you and Mendes are out of sight you shouldn't see them. The van is on the schedule, so they won't take any notice of that. We'll be in and out before anyone's any the wiser,' Benton said picking up the paperwork for the delivery and the fake IDs.

'Won't they be armed in the guardhouse?' said Danny, looking at the Pentic rifles over on the table near the truck.

'Still as cautious as you were in Afghanistan. The two on the front desk will have sidearms, but the rest won't be armed. The guards check their weapons into a strongroom at the end of each shift; it's to the left of the front desk, here,' he said, pointing to a small room off the reception. 'Remember, they're not expecting trouble. The most interesting thing that ever happens is the odd mole triggering the sensors between the fences. They're bored and apathetic, it'll be like taking candy from a baby.'

'So when is this all taking place, in a few days, weeks?' said Danny, looking at the plans. He pretended to take note of the buildings but was really looking for a name or address to identify which facility they were targeting.

'This afternoon. The delivery is scheduled for 3 p.m,' said Benton with an unexpected grin. 'Study that lot, we leave at two.'

Danny watched him walk off to check on the others. He returned his attention to the plans and photos, calmly flicking through them while his mind raced.

Shit, I need to get that phone out of the box so Tom can track us.

CHAPTER 23

'Yes,' said Tom answering the phone halfway through the first ring.

'We've got four vans in the timeframe, two of which are possibles. The first is a white Ford Transit van, bought locally and registered to a John Smith at an empty rental address. It was last seen seven miles from Guildford on a traffic cam in East Horsley. The second one is a grey Vauxhall Vivaro, sold by the previous owner six months ago but never registered to the new one. We have it on a traffic cam, it's stationary at an address approximately five miles from your location. I'm sending the details to your phone now,' said Howard, his tone never giving his feelings away.

'How should we proceed?' said Tom.

'It's your call, Tom. If you think his cover's blown, he may already be dead. Go in hard and get him out. Good luck,' said Howard, hanging up before Tom could answer.

His phone buzzed with the incoming details before he could get it away from his ear. Looking up the address of the grey Vauxhall, Tom tapped it in the sat nav, then turned to the two armed men in the back.

'Right, guys, we've got a suspect vehicle stationary at an address five miles from here. Tell your team to keep close, we're going in,' said Tom tuning back and waving John onward. As he drove, the team's radios crackled with talk behind him as the other BMW followed closely behind.

Driving the powerful cars hard the teams covered the five miles in no time. The car behind Tom peeled off as John slowed to turn onto the road close to the van's location. They pulled to a halt fifty metres short and waited until the other team's BMW appeared, approaching in the distance from the far end of the road.

With a flash of the lights both cars disembarked. The strike teams instantly took the lead, closing in from left and right, their Heckler & Koch MP5 sub-machine guns up and prone as they approached the van. Tom and John hung back, watching the team hug the wall of the property as they slid up to the front door. There was a moment of still tension while the man at the rear moved between them. He swung a heavy door ram just below the lock, imploding it inwards in a thunderous boom, triggering the end of the stillness. The team stormed through the door, sweeping from room to room.

'Armed officers, get down on the floor! NOW!'

Tom listened to the commotion over the radio. He didn't have to wait long before, "Target secured," crackled its way over the radio. Fighting the urge to tear through the house, Tom followed the voices to the lounge at the rear of the house. When he entered, he found the homeowner, a middle-aged woman, pale and shaking in one of the lounge chairs. Two of the strike team were busy hoisting an overweight, balding man off the floor. His hands were zip-tied behind his back as they dumped him in another chair. He sat there with his bottom lip trembling and his eyes wide as they darted around the room.

'Who are you?' said Tom moving in close to the man, making him jump.

'Gordon, Gordon Riley,' the man answered nervously.

'You didn't register your van when you bought it. Why?'

The man shifted in his seat and looked nervously at a bag of tools by a radiator.

'Answer me!' yelled Tom, moving closer until he was inches from Gordon's face.

'I'm sorry, ok. I'm a plumber. I've been working while claiming disability benefit. I, eh, didn't want to register the van in case the tax office found out,' said Gordon, cracking and bursting into tears.

'Cut him loose, guys, we're wasting our fucking time here,' said Tom, turning to leave.

'So I'm not under arrest?' said Gordon, not sure whether to be scared or relieved.

Turning back, Tom looked at the shocked woman whose home had been invaided. 'Mr Riley here is going to fix your radiator for free and when he's done, he's going to pay for a new front door for you. Aren't you, Mr Riley?' said Tom fixing him with a hard stare.

'Yes, yes, of course. Anything you say,' he replied, nodding his head rapidly.

The teams left and climbed back into the cars where they waited for Tom's orders.

'Get us to the last known location of the Ford Transit, John.'

'Yes boss,' said John already pulling away, the second car following closely behind.

CHAPTER 24

A half-mile walk away from MI6 headquarters, Christopher Swash shuffled from foot to foot. He looked around nervously from the shadows under the wide railway bridge. The deep rumblings from overhead trains added to his agitation as they headed in and out of Waterloo station. A large black Range Rover moved silently up beside him. The rear window slid down, exposing General Rufus McManus's face over the one-way privacy glass. Swash's head darted left and right before he opened the door and got in.

'Christopher, what is so important it can't wait?'

'Sorry, General,' Swash said, taking a worried pause before continuing. 'I—I gave you the information about Howard and Jenkins and Tripp, like you asked.'

'Yes, you did,' said Rufus, knowing what was coming next.

'It's the money. I, I need the money, I really need the money,' he said with pleading eyes.

'Come now, Christopher, that was not the deal. I will pay off your gambling debts as agreed, in three months'

ALIVE UNTIL I DIE

time, as agreed. If Jenkins does an internal investigation regarding the leak, the first thing he'll look for is any money transfers,' said Rufus, his voice calm as he looked Swash coldly in the eyes.

'Yes, yes, I know. But I've had men at my house demanding money. They say if I don't pay them, they're going to hurt me,' Swash said, his face pathetic like a begging child.

'Mmm, have you got any information on Howard or Jenkins' investigation?'

'What? Er, no. Since Tripp's death, they've taken it out of the department. We've had internal affairs checking everyone's computers and email accounts.'

'You still have the phone I gave you to contact me?'

'Of course, it's locked in my desk at work. Now, about the money.'

'You locked the phone you contact me on in a desk in the middle of an MI6 office,' said Rufus, his voice raised as his temper rose.

'Yes, but it's locked up, it's perfectly safe. Now about the—'

'Now you listen to me, you idiot. I want you to go and get that phone and bring it back here in two hours' time. I will get you some cash to keep the debt collectors off your back temporarily, but you'll have to wait for the rest, ok?' Rufus said, calm again but with a commanding edge to his voice.

'Yes, General, thank you. Two hours, thank you,' said Swash, the relief washing over him as he opened the door and stepped out.

'Two hours. I'll be here,' he said again before closing the door.

Back inside the car, Rufus turned to his driver.

'To the office please, Hugh. Once you've dropped me

off, I'd like you to pick up Mr West and be back here for Mr Swash's return.'

'Yes sir. Any specific request, sir?' said the driver moving smoothly through the London traffic.

'Mmm, yes. Get Mr West to put the fear of God into that whining little shit. Keep him in his place.'

'Certainly sir.'

CHAPTER 25

Danny sneaked another look at his watch as he dressed in the G4S uniforms. Two o'clock was coming round fast.

'Hey, Mendes, where do you piss around here?' Danny said pulling his boots on.

'Er, oh. Just go behind the barn,' Mendes said, dismissing him with a wave.

From the other side of the barn Benton's head turned, his hand twitched slightly by his side, and his hawk-like eyes watched Danny leave the barn. Outside, Danny wasted no time. He scooted round the barn and made for the Transit van. After a quick glance behind him he circled round to the passenger side door and looked in to see the metal ammunition box in the footwell. He tried the door handle.

Damn. Locked.

He tried the side door. Also locked. Danny moved around to the rear of the van. Not expecting them to open, he tried the back doors as he went. Much to his surprise, a

STEVE TAYLOR

door opened with a slight clunking sound. Leaning back to peer around the door, he checked the barn. No one in sight. Taking a deep breath to calm the adrenaline pumping through his veins, he climbed in the back of the van.

———

Benton had turned back to his plans after Danny's exit. He tried to continue where he left off, but paranoia niggled inside him to the point where he couldn't ignore it. Instinctively, he tucked a sidearm into the back of his trousers and moved casually towards the barn door.

———

Leaning over the front seat, Danny picked up the ammunition box and put it on the seat. He opened the lid and rummaged through the phones until he found the one Tom had given him. Tapping the button on top, Danny watched the screen light up with the word 'searching' in the signal box.

Come on, how long does it bloody take to get signal lock?

———

Turning his head slowly, Benton looked along the length of the barn from one end to the other. With no sign of Danny, he turned and strolled towards the end of the barn where the Transit was parked.

———

Yes, finally!

With the signal bars near full, Danny waited a few more seconds just to make sure the phone had enough time to get a location signal out to Tom. Turning the phone off again Danny quickly dropped it back into the box and clipped the lid down.

Come on, Danny boy, you're taking too long.

Moving to the corner of the barn, Benton leaned in so just a small part of his face would be visible as he looked round. He took in the side of the barn, its hedges beyond and the parked white Transit van. No sign of Danny. His eye twitched. Flashes of a rancid piss- and blood-covered dirt floor below him as he hung from a hook on the ceiling, escaped from the place in his mind where he kept them locked away. Clamping his eyes shut he chased them away. When he opened them again he slid one hand behind him and closed it around the grip of the gun tucked into the back of his trousers. Keeping it there, he trod lightly, moving to the back of the van. He placed his hand silently on the handle and in one swift movement, clicked it up and whipped the door open.

The van was empty.

'Alright, Rex? Fuck me, that's better. I shouldn't have drunk all that beer last night, I nearly flooded the field back there,' Danny said, walking round the far side of the van while doing up his flies.

'Get yourself ready, we are leaving shortly,' said Benton, eyeing Danny cautiously, his hand still on the gun behind him as he slammed the van door shut.

Danny walked past him ignoring the look as he headed

back to the barn. Standing stock still, Benton followed Danny with his eyes until he disappeared into the barn. Half a minute later he eased his hand off the gun and walked back to join them.

CHAPTER 26

After passing the last traffic camera to see the white Transit van, Tom and his team continued in the same direction until they entered the outskirts of Guildford. With no further sightings of the van and no idea where it could have gone, Tom's worry for Danny's safety and frustration with the lack of clues grew by the second.

'Pull over, John,' he said trying to think.

He was just about to call Howard when a location alert pinged on his phone.

'Yes, gotcha!' he said, opening up the maps to see where it had come from.

'You got a signal, boss?' said John leaning over.

'Had a signal, it didn't last more than a few seconds,' replied Tom, tapping the location into the sat nav. 'Eight miles away. Let's go.'

The two vehicles took off, leaving Guildford and heading into the Surrey countryside. When they got within a mile of the location they slowed. Tom pulled up a satellite image of the location on Google Earth. He zoomed in until he could see the image of the farmhouse and barn.

'There's a lane up ahead, John, 200 metres on the left. Drive past it and pull up in the next lay-by,' said Tom turning in his chair to talk to the team leader in the back. 'Do you have the surveillance drone with you?'

'Yes sir, it's in the other vehicle.'

Tom nodded and turned back as they passed the lane leading up to the farm. They continued for a quarter of a mile along the hedge-lined country road, eventually turning into a dirt track leading up to some woodlands. The strike team wasted no time breaking out the large drone from its solid black flight case. Within seconds one of the team powered up the controller and sent the drone humming high into the air. When its sound was inaudible and it was no more than a speck in the sky, the operator guided it across the fields towards the farmhouse and the last known location of Danny's phone. Watching over the operator's shoulder at the drone's camera feed, Tom saw the farmhouse and barn from an eagle eye view.

'No sign of a van or Benton's lot,' said Tom, his eye desperately searching the small screen.

'Hold on a minute, sir, I'm switching to thermal.'

The screen changed, Showing the buildings in shades of blue running to blacks in the coldest spots. No red or yellow body-shaped hot-spots.

'Is that it, nothing?' said Tom frustrated.

'Sorry, guv, we've got no heat signatures. There's no one there.'

'Shit. Ok, bring the drone in, we'll take a look.'

They packed the drone back in the boot and the BMWs backed out of the lane and hurtled to the farm track. They skidded to a halt in front of the barn and fanned out with weapons drawn. Tom and John stayed by the car and let the team do their sweeps of the farmhouse and barn.

'Clear,' came a shout from the farmhouse, followed closely by a shout of, 'Clear,' from the barn.

'Sorry, guv, house is clear and barns empty. They were here, though. There are fresh tyre tracks from the side of the barn and larger tracks leading out of the barn. Big van or truck,' said one of the team leaving the barn.

Tom went into the barn for himself. It was empty and neat. Too neat. Nothing lying about. The concrete floor had been recently and meticulously swept.

'Right, there's nothing here. Let's wrap it up, guys,' Tom said, calling Howard's number.

'Tom,' came Howard's voice.

'They're gone. We missed them.'

CHAPTER 27

Danny and Mendes sat in silence as Kristoff drove the G4S lorry into an industrial estate in Guildford. The Transit, freshly adorned with *ACM Event Management* signage and new number plates, followed closely behind. Kristoff pulled over next to an industrial unit with a 'Let Agreed' sign on the front. Benton drove the Transit up to the large loading door, hopped out and unlocked a smaller entrance door to its right. He disappeared inside, appearing a few seconds later pulling on the chain to raise the loading door up and back on its rails. From his view in the lorry cab, Danny could just make out two cars parked deep inside the unit; he lost sight of them when Knowles drove the Transit inside. The loading door rattled back down and the two men exited, locking the unit behind them. They slid the roller door at the back of the lorry up a few feet and hopped in, closing it down behind them. Benton banged on the back of the cab and Kristoff moved the truck away from the kerb, driving out of the estate. As they moved out of the town, Danny couldn't help but feel the adrenaline-fuelled excitement and the pre-mission buzz he missed from his SAS days.

'Heads up, five minutes to target,' said Kristoff, banging on the metal behind him to signal to Benton and Knowles.

Reaching down, Danny picked up his helmet and put it on, the attached visor's tint just dark enough to obscure clear identification of his face. Mendes put his on next to him and passed the other one to Kristoff.

'Fuck, let's do this!' shouted Kristoff, slapping the steering wheel.

'Money in the bank, man, money in the bank,' replied Mendes excitedly.

They turned up a private access road and followed the high razor-wire-topped fence that surrounded Centrex research centre. The security hut and main gate in the distance got closer by the second, until they pulled up in front of the barrier. An armed guard stood on the other side, his MP5 rifle held lazily across his chest. Winding down the window, Kristoff smiled from under his visor to the guard in the security hut.

'Hi, how you doing today?' he said, leaning out to pass the fake delivery manifest and IDs through the hut window.

'Good thanks, not much excitement happens around here. You guys are bang on time today,' he replied, ticking them off against his log.

He handed the paperwork back and pressed the button that slowly raised the barrier.

'If you can just pull over in bay number one please, by the guardhouse, someone will come and escort you to your drop off point.'

'Thanks pal,' said Kristoff, pulling through the gate

and waving as the guard from behind walked back into the hut.

'Ok, here we go, guys. Get ready,' said Mendes reaching under the seat to pull the rifles out.

'Ok go, go, go!' yelled Kristoff, banging on the cab behind him the second they stopped.

With smooth synchronicity, Danny and Mendes flew out of the passenger door and burst into the office at the front of the guardhouse. Benton and Knowles pulled the rear door up and leaped down. They ran at full pelt to the hut by the gate, bursting through the door before the two guards even looked up from their chairs.

'Slide the weapons over here, easy. This is not a test or a drill. One false move and I will shoot you,' shouted Benton, his face obscured by the helmet.

'What the fuck do you think y—' one of the guards started to say defiantly.

Benton moved forward in a flash. He whipped the stock of his rifle into the man's face with terrific force. The guard's nose broke to one side, landing him flat on his back, semi-conscious. Knowles pushed the other guard onto the floor and zip-tied his hands behind his back, then hogtied him by zip-tying his ankles to his wrists. Benton did the same to the semi-conscious guard.

————

Bursting through the guardhouse doors ahead of Mendes, Danny waved his rifle around and yelled at the two surprised guards.

'Face down, on the floor now!'

As the men complied, Mendes moved past Danny and tied them up with zip ties. Leaving him, Danny moved through the door to the rest and living areas. He startled two playing pool and one on the sofa beside them.

'On your fronts, hands behind your heads. NOW!'

Staying put, they looked at him with a mixture of defiance, confusion and fear.

'I said get down now!' shouted Danny again. The sight of Mendes—a second gunman coming in, rifle in the air—convinced them to comply. Mendes and Danny moved through the room zip-tying them up.

'Security hut secure, heading for target now,' came Benton's voice over the radio.

'Where's the sixth man?' said Mendes looking around.

'I'll find him, you take out the comms room,' Danny said heading for the sleeping quarters.

Moving as quietly as he could in the body armour and helmet, Danny swung into the first bedroom to find it empty. He backed out and moved down the hall. As he turned into the second bedroom, the hairs on the back of his neck stood up. Sensing someone behind him, Danny spun round on the spot. A huge guy in shorts and a T-shirt burst out of the shower room and grabbed the barrel of his rifle, pushing it to one side with one hand he rammed Danny's helmeted head into the wall with the other one. Reacting instinctively, Danny kidney punched the man as hard as he could. The guy was in top shape, his abs solid, like hitting a brick wall. He took his hand off Danny's head to get a better hold on his rifle, twisting it out of Danny's grip. Powering his helmeted head forward, Danny bounced it off the bridge of the guy's nose with an almighty crack. The blow instantly separated the two of them. The man fell back one way and Danny staggered back the other. The rifle left both of their hands and clattered down the corridor.

'Danny, what's going on?' came Mendes's voice over his headset.

The upper hand only lasted a second as the man bolted back upright, blood pouring from his broken nose. Enraged, he grabbed hold of Danny's body armour and lifted him off the floor, throwing him back with terrific force through the door to the sleeping quarters. Danny crashed dead centre into wardrobe doors. They shattered and folded inward as Danny disappeared inside swallowed in a heap of falling clothes.

I'm getting too old for this shit.

Before he could pull himself out, hands grabbed him dragging him onto his front on the floor. Danny could feel the guy trying to rip his helmet off. Twisting he looked up and saw Mendes barreling into the room, his rifle raised ready to fire.

Don't do it, don't fucking pull that trigger.

With an almighty push, Danny threw the man over to one side. He pulled out his sidearm and clubbed the guy across the temple as hard as he could. The blow stunned him for a second, giving Danny enough time to secure him with zip ties.

'It's alright, I've got him!' Danny shouted to Mendes, relieved to see him lower his rifle.

CHAPTER 28

After tabbing to the target building in double-quick time, Benton and Knowles tapped the door entry card supplied by the fixer, Hamish Campbell, on the grey pad next to the door. The light flicked to green and the door buzzed as the magnetic locks held open. They entered a brightly lit corridor with offices leading off to the left and right. Using the plan of the building imprinted in his memory, Benton led the way towards a door at the far end. He placed the passkey on the next pad and pushed the door open when it buzzed.

The fluorescent light above his head blinked and flickered as they stepped into the corridor beyond. Benton froze on the spot. His feet felt like lead and his rifle shook in his trembling hand. Images, vivid and terrifying, took control, causing him to relive the bare bulb in the basement flickering when his capturers attached live wires to his genitals. Memories of losing control of his bodily functions as his muscles spasmed made the smell of piss and shit real in his mind.

'Guv?' said Knowles from behind him, confused at their lack of movement.

Two technicians walked out of an office into Benton's path. They jumped at the sight of helmeted gunmen, their eyes wide in fear. Benton exploded into action, striking the nearest man in the mouth with the barrel of his rifle. The power of the blow shattered the poor man's front teeth. As he went down, Benton moved forward closing in on the other man. The technicians' white lab coats morphing in his mind to the thobes worn by his ISIS capturers.

Letting his rifle swing on its shoulder strap Benton thrust his hand over the man's mouth and pushed him into the wall. With his other hand he slid a razor-sharp commando knife from its sheath and plunged it under the technician's chin, pushing it right up to the hilt. As he pulled it out, the man's lifeless body slumped to the ground. His colleague on the floor freaked out in absolute terror. He let go of his bloody mouth and tried to crawl away, slipping and sliding along the vinyl floor in the pooling blood.

With glazed eyes, Benton knelt on his back, squashing him to the floor. He reached around and slit the man's throat. Blood sprayed across the floor as he made a hideous gurgling sound. It was all over in a couple of seconds. Expressionless, Benton stood and walked on without looking back, his eyes slowly regaining their hawk-like quality as he left the corridor.

Knowles looked on in horror at the unnecessary slaying of innocent civilians. With growing apprehension, he had no option but to continue the mission. Stepping over the dead men he followed Benton into the next room. When he caught up with him, Benton was checking stencilled consignment numbers on a large four-by-three-feet flight case.

'Er, everything ok, guv?' Knowles said moving up beside him.

Benton undid the clasps and nodded to the other end of the case. 'Help me with the lid.'

They lifted it off to expose a cylindrical object looking like a small jet engine surrounded with tubes and cylinders all welded into a sturdy steel frame.

'What is it?'

'Better you don't know, Peter, better you don't know. Let's get out of here. The clock's ticking,' Benton said clicking the lid back into place.

They tapped the brake release on the case's wheels and pushed it through the warehouse to the loading door. Pressing the up button, the roller door opened to reveal the back of the G4S lorry, open and ready with Kristoff standing beside it waiting. He grinned from beneath his helmet's visor.

'On three. One, two, three,' said Benton, as they all grabbed the handles on the case and lifted it onto the truck.

'Package acquired, prepare for evac,' said Benton over the headset.

'Roger that,' crackled Mendes's and Danny's voices in reply.

Kristoff got back in the driver's seat while Benton and Knowles jumped in the back. They left the roller door up this time, in case they had to make a swift exit. As the truck moved forward, screams and shouts came from the other side of the warehouse as staff discovered the dead technicians.

'Mendes, Pearson, evacuate the guardhouse now. We'll be leaving in a hurry,' shouted Benton over the revving engine.

Kristoff swung the truck left onto the road leading back

up to the guardhouse. A blast of automatic fire tore a wavy line through the thin aluminium side of the truck. Benton and Knowles clung on hard to the straps either side of the open door, with no choice but to hope they didn't cop a bullet. When the turn was complete, two of the armed guards came into view running up the road behind them. One dropped to his knee preparing to shoot again. Benton opened up his Pentic rifle. Its high velocity bullets ripped through the man's chest almost cutting him in two. The other guard dived behind a row of metal industrial bins. Benton laid down more fire to keep the guard in place as they drove off.

Danny and Mendes were outside the guardhouse, both on one knee, rifles up. Mendes covered the exit gate while Danny covered the approaching truck. Kristoff slowed to a crawl as he passed to allow Danny to leap into the cab. Mendes jumped up and hung onto the outside with his arm through the open passenger window. He jumped down when they reached the security hut by the gate. Running in, he punched the button to raise the barrier before sprinting back out and jumping into the cab next to Danny. As Kristoff jammed his foot to the floor, Benton looked out the back at the access road, only pulling the roller door down when he was satisfied no one was following. Opposite, Knowles sat on the floor staring at him, lost in worrying thoughts.

What the hell was that about? Fucking lunatic slaughtered those civilians. This isn't what I signed up for.

CHAPTER 29

n no time at all they were back on the industrial estate. It was after working hours and the estate was all but deserted. Kristoff stopped the truck kerbside and slapped the back of the cab twice. A second later Benton and Knowles moved across the forecourt and entered the unit. Danny watched as the loading door opened and the Transit drove out onto the road. Kristoff wasted no time in driving the truck in through the door, pulling it forward as far as it would go. As they got out, Knowles was reversing the Transit inside with Benton dropping the door down behind it.

'Fuck yeah, teamwork makes the dream work,' shouted Kristoff excitedly.

'Well done, men, a successful mission,' said Benton, peeling the body armour off.

'What happened in the warehouse, guv? We heard a lot of shooting,' said Mendes.

'Two armed guards caught us by surprise and a couple of lab technicians got caught in the crossfire. A bit close for comfort wasn't it, Knowles?' said Benton, giving him a warning look.

Knowles stared back trying to decide whether to challenge Benton, causing an awkward couple of seconds' silence. 'Yeah, a bit close for comfort,' he finally said.

Carrying on, Benton moved over to a big plastic bin next to a large drum with caustic hazard stickers on it.

'Right, listen up. Grab your clothes bags out of the Transit and strip. All uniforms, gloves and helmets in this bin. Put fresh latex gloves on and clean your weapons thoroughly, then place them in the boot of the Nissan Qashqai over there.'

They went through the motions, taking extra care to clean the weapons free of any forensic evidence. Benton pumped a nauseous smelling liquid out of the drum into the plastic bin of clothes. It started bubbling and reacting on contact as the material melted away.

'Powerful stuff,' Danny said to Benton.

'Doesn't come much stronger; half an hour of that and even the helmets will be nothing more than soup. When we're done I'll spray the truck down with it, there'll be no trace of evidence,' Benton replied dragging out a container with shoulder straps and a hose feeding a spray nozzle, like one a gardener would use to spray weed killer.

'That thing, the device we stole. What is it?' Danny asked.

'It's an experimental pulse weapon, charges off a hydrogen cell, then boom. It'll fry your brain and scramble your insides if you're within 100 metres of it. It's designed to take out everyone in a building without so much as cracking a pane of glass,' Benton said without emotion.

'Jesus, what does the client want to do with it?' Danny said more to himself than asking Benton directly.

Benton put the spray container down and stood

upright. He stared into Danny's eyes with an odd, distant look on his face. Danny couldn't help but notice a slight shake in his right hand. Tension started to grow. Danny was in two minds whether to tough it out or plant a fist in Benton's face and head for the weapons in the boot of the Qashqai. The moment passed before he was forced to choose. Benton turned away and shouted, 'Knowles, Mendes, is the Transit all loaded?'

'Yes guv,' came a reply from the back of the Transit, followed by Knowles's head popping out the back.

'Ok, take it to the venue, they're expecting you. Put the weapon under the stage, just as we planned. Stack the other AV kit on the stage ready for their guy to set up tomorrow. I'll catch up with you at the safe house once I've wiped this place,' said Benton, walking over to the Qashqai. He opened the glove box and pulled out a packed jiffy bag and three brand new burner phones. He put one in his pocket and gave one to Knowles, then threw one across to Kristoff.

'Use these. The number of mine is in the contacts. We keep off our own phones until we deliver the package and dispose of the vehicles. I'll keep them until then,' he said, picking up the ammunition box with all the phones in and placing it in the Qashqai.

Something was off about Benton, Danny could sense it, and by the way Knowles was acting he knew it as well.

'Danny, you and Kristoff take this to the fixer then meet me at the safe house later. Kristoff knows where it is. Use the Astra,' he said tossing the jiffy bag over.

'It's payment for our alibi boys. While the robbery took place, we have witnesses and a digitally edited CCTV recording putting us in a snooker hall in Clapham,' Benton said upbeat with an out of character grin.

This seemed to put them at ease, so Danny played

along and cheered with the others. A few minutes later the Transit was on its way and Kristoff drove the Astra out into the early evening traffic.

Danny sat in the passenger seat watching Benton in the wing mirror. He stood in the doorway to the unit, watching them leave with his hawk-like eyes. Just before they turned out of sight, Danny saw him take a phone out of his pocket and put it to his ear. Danny sat quietly for a while, deep in thought. He was no closer to finding out who was behind this or where Mendes and Knowles were taking the pulse weapon. He eventually broke the silence and tried to get some information out of Kristoff.

'What the hell's up with Benton today, he's acting weird, yeah?'

'He's wound a little tight, that's all, don't worry about it,' said Kristoff, dismissing the subject.

'Mmm, ok. What's the deal with the fixer?'

'The client's a cautious man, everything comes through the fixer. No ties, no contact,' said Kristoff turning back onto the A3 and heading back into central London.

'Makes sense, I guess. Where are Mendes and Knowles taking the pulse weapon?' Danny said, pushing Kristoff a little further.

'Fuck's sake, Danny, what's with the third degree? I don't know where they're taking it, because I don't need to know, ok? Look, I like you, my friend, but stop asking so many questions. Trust me, it didn't end that well for the last guy,' Kristoff said, the annoyance very clear in his voice.

'Ok, ok. Fuck me, I was only trying to pass the time,' said Danny, trying to sound hurt.

CHAPTER 30

I t was dark by the time Knowles and Mendes arrived at Central Hall, Westminster. They pulled up in a loading bay by the rear fire escape doors. Knowles hopped out and pummelled loudly on the door with his heavy-duty orange latex gloves. He waited for a minute or two and was about to bang again when he heard the metallic clunk of the release bar on the rear of the door being pushed down. It opened out to reveal a short, middle-aged security guard, his ill-fitting jumper riding up on his round belly. Behind him stood a tall, skinny, young guard, his uniform obviously too big for him as it hung off his coat hanger shoulders.

'Alright mate? ACM Event Management. I've got all the kit to drop off for the press thing,' said Knowles, passing him the paperwork with a jovial smile.

'Yeah ok, son. We've been expecting you. The Great Hall is round there to the left,' the chubby guard said, barely glancing at the paperwork before pointing his podgy finger in the general direction.

'Ok, thanks guys,' Knowles said waving to Mendes.

'You're just dropping off, yeah?'

'Yep, your in-house AV guys, White Light, are setting it all up,' said Knowles opening the other door to let Mendes through with a large monitor speaker.

'Ok, help yourselves, we'll be on the front desk. Give us a shout when you're finished,' the guard said, already walking away uninterested, waving the younger lad away with him.

'Ok, thanks buddy.'

They watched the security guards intently as they wandered off down the corridor. Once they'd gone, they got on with unloading the boxes and flight cases, carrying and wheeling them through to the Great Hall. They stacked them on the stage of the huge circular hall with its ornate domed ceiling and huge organ pipes left over from its days as a central London Methodist church. Double-checking the corridors, they wheeled the last large flight case containing the pulse weapon through the double doors to the Great Hall.

Pushing and pulling the heavy case, they moved it down the side of the stage to a small locked door leading to the storage area underneath it. Mendes pulled a glasses case out of his pocket and flipped it open. He fumbled to get a set of lock picks out, struggling to get a grip in the heavy-duty gloves. While Knowles kept an eye on the entrance doors, Mendes took a knee and slid the picks into the lock, clicking the pins one at a time until he could turn the barrel and open the door. He flicked the light switch, illuminating a large, low-ceilinged, dusty storage area full of crates and props and lights, and boxes full of Christmas decorations. They manoeuvred the flight case carefully through the tight doorway, stooping as they pushed, moving things out of the way until they managed to get it to the back wall.

'Miguel, go and keep an eye out for those two clowns,' said Knowles, unlocking the catches and lifting the lid.

'Ok, make it quick, yeah?' Mendes replied, taking care not to bang his head on the stage beams on his way out.

Knowles tapped a number code into the built-in stainless-steel keyboard attached to the side of the device. The ten-inch LCD touchscreen powered into life above it. He pressed the red button labelled p*rime power source*. A series of servo motors opened valves to the hydrogen tanks at the rear of the device. The button turned green and the text changed to *fuel cell primed*. Knowles continued through the menu, punching in another code to arm the device. When the red *armed* light came on, he connected a ribbon cable from the keyboard to a mobile phone cable tied to the side of the machine.

With the weapon all set, Knowles pulled a plastic zip-lock bag out of his pocket. He took two pieces of clear tape out, peeled them apart and pressed the centre onto the touchscreen. Peeling it back, he could just make out the fingerprint of Abdel Belhadj's brother, Jarrel, through the screen's glow. Tucking his hand in the bag again, he pulled out a tiny paper envelope. Turning it upside down, he shook out three of Jarrel's hairs inside the flight case. Satisfied, he closed the lid and clicked a padlock through each clasp on the outside of the case. Making sure the bag, envelope and piece of tape were safely back in his pocket, he pulled boxes of Christmas decorations in front of the device and made his way out. Turning the light off, he clicked the door shut behind him and nodded across to Mendes still keeping watch, half-in and half-out of the entrance doors. Knowles gave the door a kick to make sure it was locked, then moved into the corridor with Mendes. They wandered casually to the front desk and found the odd-looking security duo sitting behind the front desk, dunking ginger nuts into large mugs of tea.

'We're all done, boss,' said Knowles.

'Oh, ok. I'll see you out,' said the older guard, putting his mug on the table and brushing biscuit crumbs off his ample belly as he got up. Leading the way, he pushed the door release bar, let them go through and then slammed the fire escape door behind them.

At the van Knowles looked both ways before bobbing down, He unscrewed the number plate and swapped it for a new one. As he moved to the back to change the rear one, Mendes pulled off the magnetic *ACM* signage and threw it in the back of the van. Both finished, they got back in. Mendes started the Transit and headed off into the night.

'Payday's coming, Miguel, time for a long holiday,' Knowles said with a grin.

'*Si*, my friend. I think now would be a good time to see my family in Mexico.'

'A very good time indeed, mate. Come on, let's get this van to the lockup and get ourselves to the safe house.'

CHAPTER 31

With sirens wailing and intense blue lights strobing from behind the grills, Tom gunned the BMW down the private road that followed the facility's high fence, the other BMW hanging on their bumper close behind. Weaving his way through the police and forensic vehicles at the gate, Tom flashed his MI6 ID and entered the gate, pulling up next to Howard's Land Rover parked by the guardhouse. Watching them arrive, Howard wandered out and waited for Tom to join him.

'Good evening Tomas, let's take a walk,' Howard said, moving away out of earshot of the police and CID outside the guardhouse.

'I take it there's no doubt it's them, boss?'

'Five men with automatic rifles firing armour-piercing rounds. Sound familiar?' Howard said walking them down towards another group of forensic police in white paper overalls. They worked methodically beyond a taped-off section, moving in and out of a white crime scene tent erected over the shot guard.

'At least there were five of them. It means Danny's still got their trust,' Tom said, relieved.

'So it would seem, Thomas. That may be the only redeeming factor here, especially as they've just stolen an experimental pulse weapon with the capability of scrambling the brains of everyone in a building the size of the O2,' said Howard turning the corner and leading Tom in through the loading bay and into the warehouse.

'Have we got any leads on the truck or the Transit?'

'No, Edward's got everyone on it, but there're no sightings on any traffic cam or CCTV so far.'

'Damn these guys are good,' said Tom following Howard to the back of the warehouse.

Howard opened the door into the corridor. He stood aside so Tom could see the two murdered technicians lying on the floor, the pooling blood bright and crimson on their crisp white coats.

'Not as good as they should have been, dear boy. What professional would slaughter two unarmed civilians,' said Howard with an unusual amount of anger in his voice.

'My, my, what have we here? A rather nasty business, if I say so myself,' came a voice from behind them.

Howard and Tom turned to face General Rufus McManus.

'General, I wasn't expecting to see you here,' said Howard, returning to his mild-mannered self as he moved forward and shook his hand.

'Well, if you remember, our esteemed Prime Minister left Project Dragonfly fully operational until your little band of reprobates get themselves into shape. I think this little adventure would come under my jurisdiction of extreme threats to national security, don't you?' Rufus said with a smug smile and an air of arrogance.

'Absolutely, Rufus, let me know if I can be of any

assistance,' Howard said with a friendly smile, not rising to the bait.

'I doubt that will be necessary, but thank you anyway,' said Rufus turning to leave. He stopped at the door and turned back. 'Will you be at the PM's little press announcement on security reform Monday?'

'No, I'm afraid I have a prior engagement,' Howard said, still keeping his composure.

'Mmm,' replied Rufus with a frown, before turning and leaving without saying any more.

'That guy's such an arsehole,' said Tom.

'Now, now, Thomas. The General's just a dinosaur who doesn't know he's extinct yet.'

The General marched out of the building and made his way to his car. Climbing in the back, he closed the door behind him.

'Has Benton checked in yet, Hugh?' he said to his driver.

'Yes boss. He said the package is in place and the targets are en route. Mr West's team is in situ awaiting their arrival.'

'Good, and the delivery team?'

'Benton is taking care of them personally,' said Hugh, starting the car.

'Excellent, take me to the Britannia Gentlemen's Club please, Hugh. I think this calls for a celebratory drink.'

'Yes sir.'

Howard and Tom watched him go as they walked back up towards the guardhouse.

'I don't trust that guy,' said Tom in a low voice.

'Let me deal with the General, Thomas. You concentrate on finding Daniel and the missing pulse weapon,' replied Howard, heading for his car.

'Yes sir,' Tom said and signalled to his waiting team that it was time to leave.

CHAPTER 32

The safe house was actually a flat on the third floor of a 1950s block in Nelson Square, just off Blackfriars Road in Southwark, central London. Mendes and Knowles parked the Transit in the lock-up garage as Benton had told them to. Walking the short distance along Blackfriars Road in good spirits, they stopped to pick up celebratory beers and a selection of Domino's pizzas. They walked past the park and tennis courts surrounded on all sides by the four seven-storey blocks of flats. When they reached the one on the furthest side, their body language changed. Even in celebratory mood they moved past the block casually checking for prying eyes or a shadowy tail stalking them unseen in the park behind. When none presented themselves they circled back and entered the foyer. Taking the stairs to the third floor, they moved silently to the door of the safe house. Making no noise, Knowles gently placed his ear on the door and listened. Oppressive tension built until the pounding of his own heart seemed to be the only thing he could hear.

'All clear,' he said in a low hush to Mendes.

Turning the key in the lock, they entered the dark hallway of the flat. Mendes flicked the light on and took the beer and pizzas into the kitchen to find some plates. Knowles wandered through to the small lounge. It was dark and gloomy, illuminated only by the jaundiced orange glow through the curtains from the streetlights below. He flicked the light switch, frowning when the lounge didn't burst into light. His eyes, becoming accustomed to the gloom, picked out a barely visible figure sitting in the darkest corner of the lounge. Seeing the silhouette of the silenced pistol, Knowles tensed, the realisation of his fate burned into his mind.

'Motherfuc—'

Three fast pops silenced him where he stood. He dropped to his knees, a textbook two bullets to his chest and one in the forehead. He stayed up for a long second before the muscles in his body realised the brain was dead and allowed him to fall with a soft thud face down onto the carpet.

In the kitchen Mendes had his back to the door as he dished out hot pizza onto plates for him and Knowles. He chucked the spatula into the sink and froze at the reflection in the stainless-steel bread bin.

Shit!

He never got to turn. The bullet entered the back of his head and exited through the front, covering the wall and pizzas in a shower of blood, bone and brains. Before Mendes's limp body slumped to the floor.

The gunman stood in the doorway, dressed in black. The bottoms of his trousers gaffer-taped to his boots, and the cuffs of his jacket taped similarly to his latex-gloved hands. His eyes burned through the holes in the balaclava over his head. Laying the silenced handgun on the kitchen table, he pinched the top of the plastic bag covering its grip, pulled it gently off and put it in his pocket. Leaving the gun where it was, he bobbed down on his haunches and went through Mendes's pockets. Retrieving the lock up and Transit keys, he stood. His hand shook slightly as he put them in his jacket pocket.

Backing out of the door, he took a last look at Knowles lying on the lounge floor. Nightmare images flashed through his head and kept him there for a while, his inner demons rooting him to the spot. Eventually the tension left his body. He opened the flat door and poked his head out into the corridor. With no one in sight, he pulled the bala-clava off and stepped out, shutting the door behind him.

Benton's head was wet with sweat. He ripped the gaffer tape from his wrists and ankles and pulled the gloves off, stuffing it all in his jacket pocket he walked casually to the stairs. Stopping in his tracks when he heard voices, Benton peeped over the bannister. From his angle above he could see a hand appearing on the bannister, and a foot working its way up the first-floor steps. The voices suggested a man and a woman, watching and listening as they moved up to the next set of stairs. Benton edged up towards the fourth floor, not wanting to be seen in the building. Before he got there, the hand and foot disappeared and footsteps echoed away down the second-floor corridor.

Benton waited until he heard the door of a flat close before moving down the stairs, upping the pace as he went. He was out the front door and away through the cover of the park moments later. A short walk and he turned onto Blackfriars Road and made a call.

'It's me. The delivery crew has been dealt with. I'm coming in.'

The recipient hung up without reply. Benton pocketed the phone and crossed the road. He checked the area and checked again before climbing into the Qashqai and driving off

CHAPTER 33

Far across the city in East Barnet, north London, Kristoff drove between the rows of terraced and semi-detached family homes along Hampden Way. Glimpses of the lights in Brunswick Park flicked into view periodically between the gaps of end terrace properties. They moved onto Osidge Lane, then turned into the empty car park at the top of the park.

'Well this doesn't look dodgy, does it?' Danny said sarcastically.

'What are you talking about?' Kristoff said, frowning at him.

'Two grown men sitting in an empty car park, by a park, in the middle of the night! Waiting to meet another man! Just saying,' Danny said with a grin.

'He's not meeting us here, you idiot, he's in the house over there,' Kristoff said, pointing across the road.

They got out. Danny followed across the road behind Kristoff who was carrying the jiffy bag. He went up the path leading to an Edwardian bay windowed townhouse.

Danny saw the front door open in front of Kristoff. Something was said just out of earshot, then Kristoff went inside. Danny followed, shutting the door behind him. He turned into the living room and came face to face with Hamish Campbell. He looked exactly as Danny remembered him: long, scruffy ginger beard with equally long, curly ginger hair that had been left untouched for so long it formed dreadlocks. His face fell at the sight of him. Danny and Edward had busted him for aiding and abetting terrorist Marcus Tenby in a cyber-attack on London a few years ago.

In a panic, Hamish pulled a Glock 17 out of the back of his jeans. Shaking, he stepped back, darting the gun between Danny and Kristoff.

'Fucking MI6, I'm not going back inside again. Now fucking back up!' he shouted, his wide eyes jumping from one man to the other like he was watching a tennis match.

'What the fuck you talking about, Hamish? We've got your fucking money. Now put the gun down before you hurt yourself,' said Kristoff, throwing Hamish the jiffy bag.

'He's MI6. I should know, I spent four years in Belmarsh because of that bastard. For all I know you're a fucking spook as well,' Hamish said, waving the gun about. He held the jiffy bag in the other hand and gripped the top between his teeth so he could rip the top off. When he looked inside, his face contorted in an angry frown. He turned it upside down and shook out the bundles of note-shaped magazine cuttings.

'What the fuck is going on?' Kristoff said, staring at the paper on the floor.

A flicker of a red laser dot appeared, then disappeared, then appeared again on the side of Kristoff's head as it negotiated its way through the half-open window blinds.

'Kristoff, get down, NOW!' Danny shouted. A hail of suppressed automatic fire ripped Kristoff to pieces, blowing him off his feet before he could react.

Danny instinctively launched himself forward, rugby tackling Hamish to the ground. The room exploded around them as the bullets from several silenced weapons tore it apart. Glass and wooden splinters flew about with the stuffing in the sofa as bullets passed through and embedded themselves in the walls all around them.

'Give me the gun,' Danny shouted over the hammering taps.

'It's not real, it's a replica. I'm not going to do five to ten for carrying a firearm.'

'Fuck's sake, move. To the back door, on your belly,' Danny shouted, pushing Hamish into the hall.

They'd just scurried out into the kitchen when a flash-bang exploded in the lounge behind them.

'They're coming in. If you want to live, stick close to me and do as I say. Now get down by the sink,' Danny shouted at Hamish's pale, shocked face.

He got to his feet and pulled the back door inwards, folding himself against the wall behind it. A stream of white hot bullets whizzed through the opening, rocking the large American style fridge freezer opposite as they punched countless holes in its brushed steel doors. Danny turned to look away from the door, his eyes falling on the knife block sitting on the kitchen counter. He slid the knives out one by one, tossing them to one side until he found one the right size and weight.

The second there was a break in the fire, Danny darted his head around the door then back again. The gunman reloaded and let rip through the kitchen window, showering millions of glass crystals on top of Hamish as he crouched, shaking. Danny swung around the door and threw his arm forward in a powerful flick. The knife spun through the air towards the locked-on target, striking the darkly clad figure in the Adam's apple. Dropping his rifle, he spun wildly around and fell to the floor clutching the handle of the kitchen knife buried up to the hilt in his neck.

'Come on, go. GO!' Danny said, grabbing Hamish's jacket and throwing him out the back door.

'Get over the fence,' Danny yelled over the sound of the front door being kicked in.

He let Hamish go ahead as he stooped down by the man on the floor. He was coughing blood out of his mouth as he struggled to breathe. Danny pulled a handgun out of his holster and picked up the C8 carbine rifle off the floor. Swinging round, he unloaded the magazine through the kitchen window and down the hall, striking a gunman as he came in through the front door.

That'll keep the bastards' heads down.

Dropping the empty weapon, Danny charged after Hamish, who was swinging his leg over the top of the garden fence. Time being of the essence, Danny shoulder-charged the fence, blasting it in two in a shower of wooden slats. He caught up with Hamish stumbling and tripping through the undergrowth at the bottom of the house behind the one they'd just left.

'Come on, move faster,' shouted Danny.

Grabbing Hamish under the arm and dragging him out of the bushes, Danny pushed him around the front a modern garden office just as bullets ripped through the undergrowth and blew splinters and chunks out of its side. A bullet tore through Danny's jacket, carving a gouge across his arm before he could tuck behind the safety of the heavy timber office building. Looking back between fire, Danny could see three men leaving the house's kitchen, all dressed in black ops kit. They moved in formation, professional, trained, and heading in his direction.

Who are these guys? What's more important is, who sent them?

CHAPTER 34

Shielded by the man in front as he took the brunt of Danny's volley of fire, Lucas West flattened himself against the front of the house until it stopped.

'Lenny, Tucker, on me. Barnes, take the vehicle round the back of this lot, Ferney Road,' West said over the head mics.

'Yes guv,' said Barnes grabbing the dead man under the armpits and dragging him away.

The three ducked into the house, sweeping the living room quickly before heading through the kitchen.

'Kristoff is terminated; Pearson and Campbell are on their toes,' West said as the three of them peeled out the back door.

They fanned out and took a knee. West clicked on the night sight attached to his rifle. Through the green glow and high-pitched whine he spotted Danny and Hamish by a garden building on the property to the rear. He pulled the trigger, and the silenced automatic rifle spat out a stream of bullets. They ripped splintered chunks out of the garden office in the space where Danny had been a split-second earlier.

———

Heading across the lawn, Danny and hamish's movement set off the outside security lights attached to the house.

'Oh shit, we're going to die,' Hamish said, his eyes wide and scared as he kept swinging his head behind him, expecting to feel the pain of a red-hot bullet at any minute.

'No, we're not. Over there, go down the side of the house,' said Danny trying not to shout.

The kitchen door opened as they passed. Reacting to the noise, Danny had his handgun trained on the owner standing in the doorway in a flash.

'I—I—I'm warning you, get away, I've called the police,' he said weakly, unconvincingly puffing his chest out and standing on his toes as he desperately tried to look bigger and scarier than he actually was.

'Get back in the fucking house, lock the door and keep away from the windows. NOW!' Danny yelled through gritted teeth, his stare dark and menacing.

The man flinched at the sight of the gun and then withered at the look on Danny's face, fear and confusion keeping him rooted to the spot as he watched them disappear down the side of the house. Noises from the bottom of the garden made him look. The sight of three darkly clad gunmen bursting out of the undergrowth shook him into action. He slammed the back door, taking a second to lock it with shaking hands. Running into the hall, he cowered on the stairs, clutching a golf club close to his chest.

'Norman, what's all that noise?' came his wife's voice from the bedroom.

'Stay there, darling, don't come down. Just stay there,' he said, almost crying.

Hearing a car approaching on the road ahead of them, Danny picked up the pace. He flew past Hamish, hurdled the low brick wall at the front of the house and landed in the road under the illumination of the approaching car. Danny levelled the gun at the windscreen and stuck his other hand up to stop it. The tyres locked up on the tarmac, sliding the shiny black 4x4 to a stop inches from Danny's legs.

To both their surprise, Danny and Barnes stared at each other. While Hamish watched from the kerb, Barnes slammed his foot on the accelerator, knocking Danny onto the bonnet as the car accelerated down the road. Holding onto the windscreen wiper with one hand, Danny hooked his gun around to the driver's side window and fired off three rounds in quick succession. The glass imploded into the car as the bullets passed through, catching Barnes in the head. As Barnes's body slumped to one side, the car swerved onto the pavement, crashing to a stop as it ploughed into a bunch of plastic wheelie bins. The sudden stop sent Danny flying off the bonnet into a front garden. He rolled across the soft turf, using the momentum to spring to his feet. Running back to the car, he yanked the driver's door open and dragged Barnes out onto the ground.

'Hamish, get in!' he shouted back down the road.

Patting Barnes down, Danny pulled two full magazines out of his tactical vest and tucked them in his jeans. Jumping in, he stuck the car in reverse and dragged it out of the bins. Putting it in first, Danny accelerated away. The rear windscreen exploded as bullets whizzed between them at supersonic speed, destroying the rear-view mirror and punching neat round holes in the front windscreen as they exited the vehicle.

Hammering his way through the gears with his foot to the floor, Danny glanced in his wing mirror to see three gunmen move out of the road and melt away into the darkness of the front gardens. Sliding the car sideways around the corner, Danny kept the speed up until they had weaved through the suburban housing estates. Satisfied nobody was following, he jammed on the brakes and slid to a halt. Ducking his hand behind him, Danny had the gun out of his belt and pointed at Hamish's head in a flash.

'You're going to tell me everything you know. Starting with who the fuck is trying to kill us,' he said, his voice raised but controlled and his face as hard as granite as he stared intensely at Hamish.

'Whoa, I don't fucking know. Look, they were trying to kill me too, so we both got screwed,' replied Hamish, shrinking up against the passenger door, trying to get as much space as possible between him and the handgun.

Neither of them moved for a while, both running through options in their mind; Hamish's to jump on a plane and disappear, Danny's to find out who was after him and kill them.

'Who do you work for?' Danny eventually said, lowering the gun.

Relaxing a little, Hamish straightened in his seat. 'I don't know his name. I was serving a ten-stretch in Belmarsh after your lot busted me for arms dealing to that bunch of psychos working for Marcus Tenby, when this suit breezes in, all mysterious like. He says he works for the security of the UK and if I work for him, he can get me out of there.'

'What did he look like?' Danny said.

'Blonde hair neatly cut short, blue eyes. Proper toff, Oxford type. Fucking arrogant twat.'

'How did you work for him?'

'He'd give me instructions through encrypted mail. They sent anything Benton needed to various parcel drop boxes. I'd pick it up and pass it on.'

'And the house back there?' Danny said, tucking the gun back into his belt.

'I was just told to meet you there. Key's under the mat, collect payment and leave,' Hamish said shrugging.

'Ok,' was all Danny said. He put the car back into gear and drove off in a more sedate fashion.

'So what's the plan then?' said Hamish, still keen on making a break for the nearest airport.

'We're going to get some answers,' said Danny with a look that said the conversation was over.

CHAPTER 35

n the heart of Westminster, Benton turned down the slope leading under the modern office building. He pulled up to a metal barrier, lowered the window and looked into the lens above the intercom. The barrier lifted silently without him having to press the intercom. Driving the Qashqai through the grey concrete car park made the harsh fluorescent lights strobe, hurting his eyes as he passed underneath them.

Benton pulled into a bay at the far end of the car park. He got out and stood next to the car with one hand on the door, ready to shut it. But he didn't; he stood locked in place by the increasingly frequent nightmares that transported him back to the tortuous, stinking basement in all-consuming vivid detail. The bare bulb, knocked by one of his tormentors as they beat him, swung from the ceiling and blinded his half-closed swollen eyes. Fighting to get back into reality, Benton forced his shaking left hand onto the door frame. With gritted teeth he slammed the car door on his right hand. The intense pain drove the horrors away, leaving him breathing heavily in a cold sweat.

When the pain dulled to a low throb, Benton walked over and looked into the camera above a heavy metal door. The light went from red to green as the facial recognition software released the lock. He bounded up the stairs, repeating the same camera recognition to enter the ultra-modern offices of Project Dragonfly.

'Welcome back, Commander,' said a pretty blonde on reception.

Benton acknowledged her with a curt nod and walked towards the command centre at the far end of the office.

'I want a status report on West and Alpha team,' he ordered, coming to a stop before a massive wall of screens.

'Ah, Commander, good to see you. I hope there were no problems your end?'

Benton turned to see General McManus striding across the office towards him. 'Evening, General. What do you mean by problems my end?'

'It would seem Mr Pearson's reputation from his regiment days wasn't exaggerated.'

'What's happened?'

'He killed three of Alpha team and escaped in one of their vehicles,' said Rufus waving to one of his minions behind a desk.

The geeky-looking man floated his fingers across his keyboard, bringing a screen to life with a recording of Ferney Road from Brunswick Park. Zoomed and digitally enhanced, Benton watched as it showed Danny riding on top of the bonnet, shooting Barnes before the car crashed. His hawk eyes darkened as he watched Danny get in the car while Hamish Campbell appeared out of the shadows to get in the passenger seat.

'Where are they now?' he said coldly.

'We've been tracking the car for the last forty minutes. It's not far from here. The car turned into Old Eye Street five minutes ago and has been stationary ever since. Alpha team are en route, ETA two minutes. I've dispatched three other teams to the area. We should have them soon,' said Rufus with his usual pompous confidence.

'Mmm, don't underestimate Pearson, he's a tough bastard. What's the situation at the house?'

'Project Nightingale has taken control of the investigation. I've warned off the Met and Secret Services, and we've got a clean-up crew on site as we speak,' said Rufus.

'Good. Get me a car, I'm going into the field. Who have we got here?'

'Grimes and Newton,' Rufus said turning away and ordering someone to get a car ready for Benton.

'Someone get me a radio and a gun. I want to be on the road in three minutes. And find Pearson and Campbell, they have to surface somewhere

CHAPTER 36

'Thank you, Jarvis, put it on my account,' said Howard, passing a twenty-pound note to Jarvis discreetly as they shook hands.

'My pleasure, sir,' said Jarvis, sliding the note into his suit jacket as Howard took the receipt off a little silver plate.

'Thank you, Howard. It's been a most productive evening,' said Minister of Defence William Pringle as Jarvis helped him on with his coat.

'I am, as always, happy to help, William. I'm not so sure General McManus will see your national security reforms in a favourable light though.'

'General McManus is an arrogant pig. The sooner we retire him and his bunch of Neanderthals the better,' said William, his pale face flushing as he worked himself up.

'Ah well, that, dear boy, is for you to sort out,' said Howard walking down the steps of the Britannia Gentlemen's Club. He waited at the bottom for Pringle to come beside him.

'Will we be seeing you at tomorrow's press release?'

'Mmm, General McManus asked me the same thing. But no. Central Hall full of press is a little more public than I'd prefer. Too many cameras, too many questions,' said Howard, raising his eyebrows.

'Fair enough.'

'Can I drop you anywhere?' said Howard, waving a hand to his driver parked up the road.

'No thanks, I'm staying at my London apartment tonight. It's only a five-minute walk and I could do with the fresh air.'

They shook hands and parted. Howard waited for his car to pull up slowly beside him. He got in the back without looking up, engrossed in the messages on his phone.

'Home please, Frank.'

When he got no response, Howard looked up to see a gun aimed at his head. Danny's face, dark and brooding, was staring at him from behind it.

'Good evening, Daniel. Whilst I'm moderately glad you're still alive, I would appreciate you not pointing a gun in my face.'

'Is that him?' Danny said to Hamish without taking his eyes off Howard.

'No. It's not him,' said Hamish, his scruffy beard and dreadlocked ginger hair flopping over as he looked round from the passenger seat.

'Now that you're suitably reassured I'm not who your homeless-looking friend thought I was, I would like to know what you've done with my driver. Because if anything has happened to him, I will have you killed,' replied Howard, his voice still pleasant, his manner dismissive of the two men in the front.

Danny continued to stare at him while he thought the situation over.

'Frank's in the boot,' Danny finally said.

'Er, Danny,' came Hamish's panicky voice.

'What is it?' Danny said, turning to see Hamish staring out the front window.

'I think it's time to go,' Hamish said slowly.

Danny followed Hamish's eye line to see two blacked-out Range Rover Sports pulling up some distance away on either side of the road. They sat there with their engines ticking over, lights bright and burning, obscuring the view of their occupants.

———

'Can I have a status report on the mobile networks?' bellowed Rufus.

'We've got access. I'm killing every transmitter that crosses Westminster now, General,' said a long-haired geeky minion, sliding his glasses up his nose as he worked furiously at his computer.

Rufus turned his attention back to the wall of screens. The two in the centre displayed a camera feed from West's car. Rufus frowned when he saw the targets in a silver BMW X7 that looked familiar.

'Who does that car belong to?' he said to the techie on his right.

'The car is registered to Oxford Financial Consultants, sir,' he replied after some lightning finger skills on the keyboard.

'That's Howard's cover company, why is Pearson there? He's one of Howard's boys. Sneaky bastard. Where's Commander Benton?' bellowed Rufus.

'One minute away, he's approaching from the rear of the target,' said the controller behind him.

'Good, patch me through to Benton and West.'

'You're live, sir.'

'Gentlemen, this is General McManus. The area is contained. The suspects have made contact with Special Operations Director Howard. It is imperative that none of these men make contact with the outside world. Do I make myself clear?'

'Crystal, General,' said Benton.

'Affirmative,' came West's voice.

'Commander, you have control,' said Rufus taking off the headset and turning back to the operatives in the room. 'I want to know everything about Daniel Pearson, everything. I want to know what he had for breakfast. NOW.'

———

Danny revved the powerful 4.4 litre twin turbo engine belonging to Howard's car. As he clicked it into drive, he caught a glimpse of a car in the wing mirror approaching from behind at breakneck speed.

'Hold on,' Danny said, stamping on the accelerator.

The big 4x4 took off like a rocket. Danny gunned it straight at the two Range Rovers in front. Their doors were opening, as black clad members of Alpha team emerged to take aim. Keeping his foot flat to the floor, the BMW X7 ate up the distance between them at an alarming rate.

'Get in!' West shouted from his kerbside seat.

The cry came too late for his man on the other side. Danny hit the car door doing fifty. It folded and smashed a gunman against the frame of the car, breaking his legs at the shins and crushing his chest against its roof. The driver opposite dived back inside as Danny passed, clipping the rear of their car on his way. A few seconds later, Benton blew through behind them in hot pursuit.

'Would anyone like to tell me who is trying to kill us?' said Howard, punching the keys on his mobile phone.

'For a minute I thought it might be you,' said Danny, raising his voice over the growling engine.

'Sorry to disappoint you, dear boy,' said Howard frowning at the lack of signal on his phone.

Before he could speak again, the back window imploded. Danny looked in the rear-view mirror to see a guy hanging out of the passenger window of the pursuing car, with a handgun pointed his way. Looking across to the driver's side, Danny's blood boiled to see Benton staring back at him.

'They've killed the mobile signal. Get across the river to the MI6 SIS building,' shouted Howard over the increased noise from the missing rear window.

'Hold on!' Danny shouted over the sound of Howard's driver screaming from the boot. He pulled the car hard around a left-hand turn. It leaned over dangerously as the tyres squealed and fought for grip. When it finished snaking to a straight line, Danny checked the mirror to see Benton's car sliding around the corner and bouncing off the kerb before accelerating after them.

146

CHAPTER 37

Outside the Britannia Gentlemen's Club, Lucas West ran across the road to the other car.

'Take Mills to hospital,' he yelled, dragging the driver out and jumping into his place. 'Get in, get in. Come on, let's go,' he yelled, pulling away before the others had shut their doors.

'Commander, this is West, what's your location?'

'We're heading north on Tufton Street, heading towards Horseferry Road,' came Benton's voice over his earpiece.

'On my way. Delta team, status report.'

'Two minutes, guv. We're heading east along the river on Grosvenor Road.'

———

'Fold the split-seat down and let Frank out,' yelled Danny to Howard.

Howard pressed the release and flopped the seat forward. Frank's wide eyes and pale face peeked back at him. An egg-sized red lump grew off his temple where Danny had pistol-whipped him into the boot. Howard helped him into the back of the car and flipped the seat up, allowing him to sit shell-shocked in the seat.

'I'd put your belt on if I were you,' said Danny seeing Tufton Street quickly coming to an end at a T-junction. Jamming on the brakes, Danny glanced in the wing mirror to see Benton's car gaining ground. The mirror exploded from a bullet as Danny looked back ahead. They slid sideways into Horseferry Road. Danny immediately slammed his foot on the accelerator and headed for Lambeth Bridge.

'We've just got to get across the bridge and we're home free,' yelled Danny.

The second the words left his mouth he jumped on the brakes. Delta team hurtled around the corner, handbrake-turning the car sideways to block the entrance to Lambeth Bridge. The windows dropped and MP5 submachine gun muzzles aimed at the BMW. Stopping fifty metres short of them, Danny twisted round to see Benton pulling to a halt a little way behind him.

'Shit. Fuck it. Hang on.'

Danny put the car into reverse and hit the accelerator. The powerful car lurched backwards, closing the gap between him and Benton in seconds. Tensing up, Danny prepared for the impact. The big, heavy 4x4 struck Benton's car hard, folding the bonnet and wings up as the back of Howard's car bent inwards. With smoke pouring off the tyres, Danny kept his foot to the floor, pushing Benton backwards down the road until they passed the turn for Thorney Street on their right. Throwing it into drive, there was a screech of metal as the cars pulled apart and Danny took off out of sight.

'Are they following?' said Howard from the back.

'No, I think Benton's car is out of action. There'll be

more of them though. I need to get somewhere I can fight them on my terms.'

————

Getting out of the wrecked car, Benton, Grimes and Newton squeezed into the back of Delta team's 4x4 and hurtled down Thorney Street after Danny.

'West, we're heading north along Thorney Street, what's your location?' said Benton over the headset.

'We're running parallel to you on Marsham Street, Commander,' came West's reply.

'Get ahead of us and cut them off on Millbank.'

'Roger that.'

————

Taking a sharp turn near the end of Thorney Street, the bright Xenon headlights gave Danny the answer he was looking for. Ahead of them lay a high office block surrounded by boarding while it was under renovation. Spotting the site's entrance gates, Danny veered towards them, hitting them hard and centre. The force on the padlocked chain pulled the metal edge off one of the gates as they blew inwards, making a loud crash as they folded back on themselves and hit the site's wooden boarding. Locking the brakes up, Danny slid to a halt by the entrance doors. Out of the car in a flash, Danny covered the gates with his gun up and level, his dark eyes unwavering along the sights.

'Everyone out, quickly get inside,' he said, swinging round to put a bullet through the large glass panel in the entrance door. The tempered glass exploded into a million crystallised pieces. Swinging back, Danny covered the gate again. Hamish, Howard and Frank stepped through the frame into the building's foyer. Danny moved backwards, still covering the gate until he was at the door, then ducked inside behind them. The stairwell and foyer lights were on, as were the lights on the lift's display panel.

Not knowing what to do, the others waited for Danny's lead. He walked past them and press the lift call.

'Go to the top floor, find somewhere to hide and don't come out until I come for you,' he said looking at his gun with a creased forehead. 'Here, take this. Anyone other than me turns up, shoot to kill,' he said handing Howard the gun and spare magazines from his jeans pocket.

Howard knew better than to argue with Danny, so he took the gun and herded the others into the lift. When the doors shut, Danny watched the numbers counting up the floors to the top, then headed off up the stairs. He put his head in the doors on the first, then second floors. They were nearing the end of refurbishment. When he reached the third floor, it was more of a building site. A snaking yellow cable hung from nails and hooks, with bare bulbs attached at intervals giving out a dim light throughout the floor. Materials and bags of plaster sat on a pallet with a pump-up pallet lift slid under. Moving over to the window, Danny looked down to see two black Range Rover Sports pulling in through the gates.

They parked short of Howard's car. The doors opened fast and the men inside fanned out with rifles up, covering Howard's vehicle and building's entrance. Danny's eyes narrowed at the sight of Benton leaving the vehicle.

Nine armed men. Not good odds.

He turned to look at the pallet stacked with heavy bags of plaster. Moving swiftly, he grabbed the handle of the lifter and pumped it until the pallet was off the ground. Putting all his body weight into the stack, he pushed with all his might. The wheels moved, gaining speed as he pushed the stack across the smooth concrete. He launched it at the large glass window. The weight of the plaster bags shattered the double glazed unit as the load toppled out into the cold night air. Catching the frame to stop himself following it, Danny leaned out and watched in slow motion as the 25kg bags spread out, accelerating towards terminal velocity on their downward journey. They crashed to the ground in thunderous dust explosions. One landed square on the head of one of Benton's men, snapping his neck and killing him instantly as it crushed him to the floor in a massive dust cloud. Another caught a man on his shoulder, snapping his collarbone and tearing his shoulder out of its socket. Blinded by the clouds of plaster, the men scattered, coughing and wheezing as they made for the entrance to the building. As a cool night breeze cleared the dust, one man remained in the middle, his head tilted back, staring up defiantly.

Benton's eyes met with Danny's, the two of them steely-faced and determined. Benton eventually looked forward and walked towards the entrance to the office block.

Two down, seven to go. Better odds.

CHAPTER 38

Kicking back into action, Danny scouted around and found a large metal lockbox in the corner. Noting the heavy padlock, he moved on towards the rear stairwell. Sticking his head out, he looked down the centre void to see the ground floor. He could see the shadows of men moving just out of view and hear doors on the ground floor opening.

Standard procedure. They'll stick to training and sweep each floor on the way up.

Turning back he spotted a large ten-pound hammer in the corner of the room. Grabbing it, Danny hurried back to the lockbox. It took a couple of swings before the padlock body popped off and bounced across the floor, leaving its U-shaped metal top dangling through the lock. Sliding it out, Danny opened the box and smiled at the sight of power tools, screws and nails inside. Pulling out a large toolbox, he turned it upside down, emptying its contents on the floor. Flipping it upright, he started loading it with items from the lockbox.

Back at the stairs, Danny cautiously looked over the bannister. He could just make out the shadows of two men passing under the lights on their way up. Leaning back out of sight, Danny heared them go through the office door on the floor below. He pictured them in his mind either side of the door, one sweeping in to cover as the other followed closely behind. When he was sure they'd moved on, he descended the stairs, light-footed and quiet. Darting his head across to see through the glass in the office door, he located the two men with their backs to him as they swept forward checking the various rooms in the dim light from the city outside. Danny took a few deep breaths to control the adrenaline pumping through his veins, then slipped silently into the office.

When the hunters are hunting, the last thing they expect is to be hunted.

Moving low, Danny headed towards them, spinning into a long office that ran parallel to the main room as the rear man turned and looked back. Going as fast as he could without making any sound, Danny reached the spot parallel to Benton's men on the other side of the thin, tin-strutted plasterboard partition wall. He swung the power tool hanging on his back by a piece of electrical flex up and grabbed it. Placing his ear against the wall, he reached forward and tapped softly on the plasterboard wall, barely loud enough to hear. With his eyes shut, the hairs on the back of his neck rose. He pictured the men on the other side turning to locate the source of the sound. He tapped softly again, knowing one would come forward while the other stood back and covered.

There it was. A boot scrape on the floor and the soft tap of the man's tactical vest touching the wall as he put his ear on the other side of the plasterboard. Raising the power tool, Danny floated it millimetres away from the board, gauging, zeroing in on his target.

There, a tap of the vest again.

Pushing hard against the wall, Danny rapidly trembled on the cordless nail gun's trigger, powering nail after nail through the soft plaster. A wheezy gurgling sound came from the other side, followed by a slump to the floor. Danny was already gone, diving to the left before rolling under a heavy oak conference table, ready for the inevitable. The second he was under, it came. Bursts of automatic fire ripped through the wall where he'd been. Within a couple of seconds, the gunman's magazine was empty. Waiting for that moment, Danny was on the move again. Pulling a long screwdriver out of one pocket and a coping saw out of the other, he charged the peppered wall, exploding out the other side in a furious display of animal aggression. The speed of his attack made Grimes falter and fumble as he tried to slot the new magazine in his rifle. Danny thrust the screwdriver up under his chin, driving it home up to the handle with one hand while burying the coping saw under his tactical vest, ripping deep into his stomach with the other. Grimes quivered and shook, his eyes wide in dying terror. Danny pushed harder and Grimes's body went still, falling straight back like a felled tree.

Danny picked Grimes's handgun up and tucked it in his jeans. Turning, he grabbed the rifle and handgun from the guy with an array of nails sticking out of his head and neck. He had a nail buried in his headset, so Danny turned and took Grimes's one, fixing it into place he made for the back stairs.

'Grimes, Wilkinson, report,' came Benton's voice over the earpiece.

'This is Newton, guv. Me and Harris are entering the second floor now.'

'Affirmative, we're on the main stairwell about to enter the third floor.'

Shit!

Danny ran for the door to the rear stairs. He could hear noise from the far end of the office, which meant they'd seen the bodies and him. Traveling at full pelt, Danny dived to the floor and slid the last five metres to the door. Bursts of gunfire tore over his head as he kicked the door open and tumbled through. Kicking the heavy fire door shut behind him, Danny flipped the lid open on a large toolbox and placed it next to the door. Picking up the plumber's gas torch inside, he taped the valve open then placed it in the bottom of the box, covering the hissing torch with the boxes of nails and screws from the tool chest. He closed the lid and teased a wire from the ignition trigger of a second torch, taped to the outside of the toolbox with its nozzle poking inside, through a hole Danny had cut.

'Grimes and Wilkinson are down, we're in pursuit heading towards the rear stairs,' said Newton over the radio.

'Roger that, we'll meet you on the third floor,' replied Benton.

Putting tension on the wire, Danny wrapped it round the door handle and turned, leaping up the stairs three at a time. To buy himself some time, Danny skipped the fourth floor and headed straight to the fifth.

'Entering the rear stairw—'

Newton's voice was cut short. The boom up the stairwell was earth shatteringly loud, instantly followed by the sound of a thousand sharp nails and screws ricocheting off the concrete, ripping their way through clothing and soft flesh. Danny could feel the building tremble under his feet as he slid into the fifth-floor office. He could hear Harris's agonising scream over his earpiece. It lasted for a minute or so before dying to a gurgling moan. Then silence.

And then there were three.

CHAPTER 39

'Christ, what the hell was that?' boomed General Rufus McManus.

'Sir, we've lost vitals on Newton and Harris,' said a techie, pointing one of the large screens on his left. Along with Grimes and Wilkinson and the others Danny had killed, Newton and Harris's images were freshly greyed out with a flatline straight and solid at the bottom where their heartbeat should go. Only Benton, West and Dexter's remained beating under their names.

'Sir, we've lost mobile lockdown. The service providers have rebooted the transmitters. It'll take ten minutes to knock them out again.'

'Leave it, they'll have backup by then. Where's The Hawk?' ordered Rufus.

'The asset is on the move, General,' came a voice from behind him.

'Patch me through.'

With the flick of a switch, background noise of a speeding motorcycle and rushing wind filled the control room.

'Hawk, this is the General. Mobile signal is live. We anticipate you only have a ten-minute window of opportunity.'

———

He bumped up the kerb and rode up to the entrance doors of a tall office block. The bright lights and tinted visor obscured any identifiable feature from the night security guard inside.

'I'll be in situ in three,' he replied from inside his crash helmet. Stepping off the bike, he beckoned the guard to the door. The second he opened it, The Hawk pulled a silenced handgun from his jacket and popped two bullets into centre mass and then one into the forehead of the shocked man. Sliding the gun away, The Hawk stepped over the dead guard and grabbed an arm, dragging him behind the reception desk. Without stopping, he walked to the lift and pressed the button for the tenth floor. The second the doors shut, he threw off the large canvas bag on his back and started removing and clicking together the components of the high-calibre sniper's rifle. He didn't remove his helmet; he could've assembled the rifle blind-folded, and the lift had a camera built into the control panel.

By the time the lift dinged and the doors slid open, the gun was locked and loaded. Moving swiftly to the south side of the dark office, he laid the gun down by the window and removed his helmet. The Hawk reached in the bag and pulled a sucker and diamond cutter out. Securing it to the window just above floor height, he spun the cutter round. With a quick tap from the butt of his handgun, the disc of glass came free with the sucker. He repeated the process with the outer pane, feeling the cold night air flowing in through the hole as he removed the cutter. Checking his watch, it was three minutes and fifteen seconds from his arrival.

Not bad.

Sliding the barrel neatly into the hole in the window, The Hawk lay down and placed his eye to the powerful sight.

'Asset in place, I'm acquiring target now,' he said with monotone calm. He tried to keep his accent neutral when he spoke, but it still managed to sneak out on certain words. Looking down at the picture on his phone beside him, it displayed the freshly sent picture of his intended target.

CHAPTER 40

Down on the third floor, the two men looked at Benton for direction. Lowering his rifle Benton stared back, his face taking on concrete hardness, the pupils of his hawk-like eyes cold and enlarged in the dark office space. He pointed to his radio pack then clicked it off. The other two followed suit and stood waiting for orders.

'Pearson,' Benton said, thinking out loud. 'He'll have taken a radio; I would, so he has. He'll want to buy time to catch us off guard, so he's two, maybe three floors above us, fifth or sixth. Me and Dexter will take the lift to the seventh and come down at him, he won't expect that. A lift is undefendable, a kill box. You come up the main stairs with lots of radio chatter. Lure him out, ok?'

'Yes guv,' said Dexter and West.

Benton moved his hand to the radio pack. The others followed suit.

'One, two, three,' he said, counting them in to click the radios on.

———

Up on the fifth floor, Danny listened intently as he gaffer-taped Grimes's handgun to one of the builders' tripod lights, that were spaced out around the bare concrete office space. He placed it behind a stack of plasterboard and lined it up to the door to the rear stairs. He flicked it to automatic and carefully attached a wire from the door handle to the hairpin trigger and moved away. Heading for the main stairwell, Danny stopped in his tracks when the radio chatter burst into life.

'West, what's your location?' came Benton's crackly voice.

'Ascending the main stairs to the fifth, over.'

Danny put his hand over the earpiece, pushing it hard to his ear to get a better listen.

'We're entering the fourth floor from the rear stairwell, over,' came Benton's voice again.

What was that? Another static crackle and the voice sounded different. Solid, not the echo from an empty office floor.

He looked at the door to the main stairs ahead of him. His forehead creased and his features hardened. In a flash Danny turned and ran towards the rear stairs.

'That sneaky bastard's gone up,' he said to himself as he carefully took the wire off the taped-up handgun and ripped it off the light. He ducked out of the office. After a quick look up and down the stairwell, he headed up, three steps at a time. Passing the sixth floor Danny continued at speed to the seventh. He flattened himself against the wall beside the door to the office space, calming his breathing and focusing his mind.

'Fourth floor is clear. Hold your position on the fifth, we're coming up,' came Benton's voice over his earpiece, clearer this time with the returning echo from the concrete stairwell.

Fourth floor, my arse.

With the rifle slung over his back, Danny crouched low and slid through the door, his handgun extended ahead of him. He reached behind him and pulled the other handgun from the back of his jeans. With both guns covering the way, Danny went for the door, knees slightly bent, feet moving quickly and silently through the empty office space. He ignored the shadows cast from the skeletal tin strut frame-worked rooms awaiting their plasterboard covering. When he reached the door to the main stairs and lifts, he slowed. He darted his head across to see through the glass panel, taking in the stairs and main landing in a fraction of a second. No one in sight. With a smooth, slow, controlled movement Danny pulled the door open and slid through, resting his hand on the door behind him to keep the tension up until it closed silently to the frame. With both guns ahead of him, he glided silently to the stair rail and peeped over. For a moment it looked clear, but on second glance Danny spotted a foot sticking out into view on the stairs between the fifth and sixth floors.

Waiting to ambush me coming out the fifth floor.

Danny reached over and stared along the gunsight, his arm solid and steady as a rock.

'Mission compromised, evacuate site immediately. You're going to have company in less than five minutes. Asset is in situ and has primary target acquired,' came a voice over the earpiece.

Danny had already squeezed the trigger before the words sank in. The sound of the Glock 17 echoed off the concrete as the bullet punched a neat hole in the top of Dexter's boot, ripping through bone, muscle and cartilage before blowing a bloody star out the bottom of his boot across the concrete. Dexter screamed and fell back on the stairs. His head moved into view as he looked straight up at Danny. Pain, puzzlement and fear rolling across it as realisation sank in. Without a flicker of emotion on Danny's face, he pulled the trigger, locking the look permanently on Dexter's face as the bullet entered the centre of his forehead. Quick as a flash, Benton's hand appeared pointing his handgun up the stairwell. He emptied the clip wildly up at Danny as he descended the stairs.

Driven back out of the way, Danny had no choice but to stay back as West followed Benton's lead, unloading his weapon as Benton went further down loading his. They repeated the process, retreating down the stairs. While the bullets ricocheted around him, the words from his earpiece finally registered.

Asset in situ, primary target acquired.

The second the firing stopped, Danny took off up the stairs as fast as he could. With his legs burning and lungs craving oxygen, he burst onto the top floor office space, just managing to duck as Howard swung an iron bar at his head.

'Whoa, it's me. Get down. NOW! Hit the fucking deck!' he yelled at Hamish and Frank standing in the middle of the empty office space.

He watched them start to duck down as if in slow motion. There was a plink as the large-calibre bullet punched a neat hole in the glass window, followed by the odd vision of Hamish and Frank flying sideways as the bullet hit Hamish in the centre of his chest, passed through his body and knocked Frank off his feet as it tore through his side. Protected by the piles of building equipment, Danny slid across the floor. He ignored Hamish, he was dead before he hit the floor. Pulling his jacket off, Danny pushed it on Frank's wound to stem the blood. Looking behind him, he could see Howard back on his phone for an ambulance. Far below them sirens wailed and strobing blue lights danced off the office ceiling.

CHAPTER 41

t took a while for the chaos and confusion to die down. Police, ambulances and armed response turned up, seeing the demolished car in the courtyard and an armed man crushed under an exploded bag of plaster next to it, they sealed the building off. It was only after Edward Jenkins and half a dozen MI6 agents turned up, closely followed by Tom and the strike team, that the site was secured and medics could get Howard's driver to an ambulance.

Danny walked out of the building, his head and upper body covered in dirt and plasterboard dust, his hands and trousers covered in Frank's blood. He grinned when he saw Tom and Edward.

'What fucking time do you call this?' he said, brushing the dust out of his unruly hair.

'I didn't want to disturb your night out with new friends,' said Tom returning the grin and pointing to the dead man on the floor.

The joking stopped as the men embraced with a quick slap on the back, then parted.

'Seriously, you ok?' Tom asked.

'Yeah, this is all Howard's driver's,' Danny replied, showing his bloodied hands in front of him.

'Any idea who these arseholes are?' asked Tom crouching down on his haunches to look at the dead man's face.

'That, Thomas, is exactly what I intend to find out,' said Howard walking past them towards Edward.

'What's more important is where Knowles and Mendes put the stolen pulse weapon. We need to find them or Benton double quick. They are planning to set the weapon off on Monday,' said Danny looking at his watch, realising it was now the early hours of Saturday morning. With his adrenaline levels dropping, exhaustion hit him like a tonne of bricks. His body sagged, and he swayed where he stood.

'Neither Benton nor Hamish Campbell know your home address, Daniel. So I suggest Tom takes you home to get cleaned up and catch a few hours' sleep,' said Howard turning to Tom. 'Take two of the strike team with you and leave them there,' said Howard pausing to look at Hamish's covered body being loaded into a coroner's van. 'We'll get an incident room up and running at headquarters. Tom will pick you up in the morning. Hopefully we'll have IDs on our deceased friends here.'

'No argument from me, I'm knackered,' said Danny, finding another piece of plaster in his hair.

Leaving the police and MI6 crime scene investigators on site, they climbed in the car and moved slowly towards the exit. Tom stopped at the broken gate to let a motorbike pass. The rider slowed as he passed, turning his head to look into the car through his blacked-out helmet. Tom didn't take much notice, but even in his exhausted state, Danny's hairs stood up on the back of his neck and his sense for trouble tingled. The pass only lasted a split-second before the rider looked forward, the large canvas bag swinging on his back as he accelerated off into the early morning darkness. Without thinking about it, Danny picked out a biro from the centre console and wrote the registration number on his hand.

'What is it?' said Tom noticing.

'Probably nothing, mate, just a feeling.'

'I know your feelings, what is it?' Tom insisted.

'Something about that motorbike rider, the way he was checking the site and us out. It seemed more than a passing curiosity. Look, forget about it. I'm knackered, I need some food and some sleep,' said Danny dismissing it.

'Ok.'

'What about you guys, you want something to eat?' Danny said turning in his seat to look at two of the strike team in the back.

'Yes, Mr Pearson, that would be good,' said one of them.

'Danny, please call me Danny. And you are?'

'I'm Curtis and this is Neil.'

'Pizza ok? There's a 24-hour place near mine and I've got a few beers in the fridge.'

'That will be fine, Mr P— Danny.'

With only a few of the capital's night shift workers and taxis shuffling the party-goers home from their boozy nights out, the journey to Danny's—including the collection of three boxes of pizzas—only took forty minutes, getting them through the door just before 2:30 a.m.

Tom headed off to get some sleep for himself, while Danny tossed Curtis and Neil a beer each and dished out the pizza. Fed and watered, Danny told them to make themselves at home while he went upstairs. He stripped and showered before diving into bed. Although he knew many men affected by the horrors they'd seen in action, sleep wasn't something that ever eluded him. He killed bad people who did bad things, end of. He took his old, not very smart phone out of the bedside drawer, turned it on and checked his messages. Two from his best friend Scott; the Minelli twins wanted a rematch. That made him smile. One from his brother Rob asking him over for a Sunday roast, and a junk call telling him he'd been in a car accident and could claim personal injury. He deleted the last, put the phone on the side and turned off the light. Within minutes he was deep in a dreamless sleep.

CHAPTER 42

'G eneral, I've got a level 5 security file on Pearson. I think you'd better take a look at this,' came a voice from one of the desks in Project Dragonfly's command centre.

Rufus turned away from the screens and marched over. He stood over the operative's shoulder, moving through the files. The further he went, the darker his mood got. When Benton and West entered the room, his eyes flicked over the top of the monitor with a burning intensity. 'Commander, just the man I want to see. Would you mind looking at this for me?' Rufus said, barely containing his anger.

Benton moved beside him and looked at the file, moving it back and forth to double check what he was seeing.

'Privately contracted to Howard's covert intelligence services. Removal of Russian Mafia family, details classified. Joint anti-terrorist mission with MI6 and the FBI, resulting in him being awarded the Presidential Medal of Freedom from the bloody President of the United States of America, details classified. He even stopped a war in the

Middle East for Christ's sake. The only thing you got right about this guy was the SAS. This is your fuck-up, Rex, you need to take care of this guy now, tonight. Take the file with you, use the addresses, find him and kill him.'

Benton grabbed the file without saying a word. He kept his hand locked onto the side of the desk so the General couldn't see it trembling. As he looked at the information on the screen, he blurred out the writing and focused on the General's reflection in the glass. The face started twisting and morphing, the image of his basement tormentors trying to surface in its place. Benton pushed back the urge to turn his weapon on the room and shoot until the magazine ran empty. The images cleared and he turned to look the General in the eye with steely determination. He nodded his acknowledgment, turned and walked away with West close behind.

'Commander,' Rufus bellowed after him.

Benton stopped and turned to face him.

'Failure is not an option. Fuck this up and there's no coming back. Do we understand each other?'

'Yes, General,' Benton said without emotion.

Leaving the room, he looked at West. 'We need to visit the armoury.'

'Hell yeah,' West said with a grin.

'We'll take the Qashqai and dispose of it afterwards,' said Benton to West as they reached the steel-meshed entrance.

'Yes, Commander, what can we do for you?' the guard said buzzing them in through the door as he grabbed the log book to sign any weapons out.

Fifteen minutes later West and Benton loaded two heavy canvas bags into the boot of the Nissan Qashqai, closed it and got in. Benton punched in the postcode on the file for Danny's last known address and drove out of the underground car park the second the sat nav loaded. Once out in the early morning darkness, he clocked the time at just past 3 a.m and put his foot down.

'We'll be there in twenty minutes,' he said.

Shuffling in his seat, West got both his Glock 17s out and checked them. He kicked the metal ammunition box in the footwell over as he moved in his seat. The lid popped open unnoticed, leaving the mobile phones visible inside.

———

Deep in sleep, Tom tossed and turned. A noise heard in his subconscious disturbed his sleep. It eventually won, forcing his eyelids open. Something had woken him, but what was it? A beep from his phone answered the question. He sat up and grabbed it, not believing his eyes. The tracking app from the phone he'd given Danny was live. It showed a pulsating red dot on a navigation map. Leaping out of bed, he flipped his laptop open and brought it up on the bigger screen. After following the direction of the phone for a couple of minutes, his eyes went wide.

'Shit, shit, fucking shit,' he said in a panic, thumbing through the contacts on his phone.

———

Curtis and Neil sat in Danny's living room watching Die Hard on the TV.

'As if. That guy's such a pussy,' said Curtis pointing his gun at the TV in a mock shot.

'It's just a film, mate, you take everything too seriously,' Neil said grinning at him.

Unheard as it vibrated silently on the work surface in the kitchen, Neil's phone buzzed frantically with Tom's

171

number. When the answerphone message kicked in, Tom hung up and rang the only other number he had.

When Danny's phone rang, he went from deep sleep to awake and answered in a second.

'Tom?'

'They're there. Get out. All of you, get out now,' Tom said fast and urgently.

Danny didn't waste time answering, he was already pulling on his jeans. Picking his gun up, he stamped his feet into a pair of trainers and moved to the window. He pulled a T-shirt on over his head while pulling the curtain back just far enough to see out the front of the house. The sight of Benton and West standing behind a car on the opposite side of the road resting an L2A1 ILAW rocket launcher on its roof as they aimed it at the house shocked him into action.

Oh, shit.

Pushing himself off the wall to gain momentum, Danny forced every ounce of power out of his legs and ran for the rear window. Hearing the thudding footsteps upstairs, Neil got up and looked out the living room window. The sight of the rocket launcher going off over-loaded his mind, locking him into a frame-by-frame view of the approaching rocket. It smashed through the window and passed over his left shoulder, striking the living room wall behind Curtis where it exploded in an all-consuming fireball of explosive shrapnel and bricks. At exactly the same time, Danny was upstairs unloading bullets into the rear bedroom window, shattering it into a million pieces as he took off feet first to jump through it.

The floorboards erupted upwards in a fire ball, surrounded by an explosion of shattering wood. The blast-wave caught Danny just as he passed through the glassless window, propelling him into the fir trees at the end of his garden. He ripped through the soft branches, swallowed by the trees, before crashing through the fence behind onto the grass of the house to the rear. Winded, concussed and temporarily deafened by the explosion, Danny lay on his back, stunned and breathing heavily.

Watching the last of the roof collapse in a fireball, Benton and West dumped the launcher tube in the boot of the Qashqai, got in and sped away. They disappeared around the corner and out of sight just as scared, confused and shocked neighbours twitched their curtains and ventured tentatively out of their front doors, mobiles in their hands as the parents called the emergency services and their kids streamed the chaos to their social media platforms.

CHAPTER 43

'Commander,' said Rufus answering his phone, still alert and sharp despite the early hour.

'General, the target has been terminated and the vehicle has been disposed of. I await further instructions,' came Benton's reply.

'Excellent. The safe house in Knightsbridge is at your disposal. Get some rest and report back here at 1200 hours.'

'Yes, General,' said Benton ending the call.

Moving forward, Rufus approached a large screen adorned with crossed-out headshots. He ran his eyes along the rows, taking in everyone from Simon Tripp and Dennis Leman to Kristoff, Knowles and Mendes. He kept going with Nikolai Korentski and Bosko Pelik, ending on Hamish Campbell and Daniel Pearson. His mouth twitched into a smile unseen by the operatives behind him. Lowering his eyes to the bottom line of photos, his expression hardened at the photos waiting to be crossed out. William Pringle, the Prime Minister and a newly added CCTV image of Howard.

'Sorry, old friend, collateral damage, you'd understand that,' he whispered to himself.

'Right, I'm off. Get some sleep, gentlemen, we still have a busy few days ahead of us,' said Rufus marching between the desks, ignoring his minions as he went.

CHAPTER 44

After the fire engines quelled the flames and the police taped off the area, Tom stood next to Howard on the roadside watching the coroners bringing out two body bags containing the remains of Neil and Curtis.

'They haven't found Daniel yet?' said Howard with no discernible emotion in his voice.

'No, not yet,' said Tom, noticeably more sombre than Howard.

'Mmm, have we put the local mob straight?'

'Yes, local plod are telling neighbours and press it was a gas leak,' said Tom gloomily.

'Chin up, Thomas, let's get back to headquarters. We still have a rather nasty pulse weapon to find by tomorrow.'

Tom walked round the car and slumped into the driver's seat while Howard sat carefully in the passenger seat, picking a bit of lint off his suit trousers before clicking the seat belt into place.

'I take it from the smell of burnt hair, my assumption

that you escaped death once again is correct, Daniel?' Howard said to Tom's surprise.

'In the circumstances, I thought it would be a good idea to remain dead,' said Danny from his position, tucked in the footwell behind the driver's seat.

'Well, I'm glad you're not, mate,' said Tom reaching behind the seat and patting Danny on the shoulder.

'Cheers, now do you mind driving? It's fucking uncomfortable down here.'

'Sure,' said Tom with a grin. He drove slowly forward, waiting for the police officer to hold the cornered-off police tape up for him to drive under. Once they were away and out of sight, Danny popped up onto the back seat.

'So what happened?' Howard said breaking the buddy chat up.

'As soon as Tom rang, I looked out the window to see Benton aiming a rocket launcher at the house. As I dived out the rear window, the bloody thing blew me into the next door's garden. How did you know they were coming?' Danny said to Tom, while feeling his singed hair.

'The tracker in the phone I gave you started transmitting. When I checked the bloody thing, it was heading straight towards your house. I left the strike team tracking it after I called you. They found the car and phone on fire two miles from here on Hackney Marshes. We had the fire brigade put it out and the wreck transported to forensics.'

'Jesus, these fuckers are really pissing me off,' said Danny, a flash of anger washing across his face.

'Quite. One would be inclined to agree with you,' said Howard, dialling a number on his phone. 'Good morning, Edward. No, no, he's very much alive. We are on our way in if you could clear our way in please. The fewer people know he's still alive, the better.'

The rest of the journey went in uneasy silence, each one of the three men engrossed in their own thoughts, each man running the events of the last few days through their minds, all still pondering the unknown question of who was behind it all. They crossed the Thames over Vauxhall Bridge, with the impressive SIS building and the headquarters of MI5 and MI6 ahead of them. Driving round the back of the building, they turned down the slope to the underground parking. Security was expecting them and lowered the ram-proof barrier into the ground. Tom drove on and parked in the bay indicated by two of Edward's men who were waiting for them. They were ushered in and up the lift, avoiding reception or signing in. For once, Danny didn't argue about taking the lift; he just stood at the back, brooding. When the door opened, Edward was there to greet them. He led the men into the newly set up incident room, stopping to hold out his hand to Danny as he departed the lift.

'Glad to have you still with us,' he said with a smile.

'Thanks, Ed. Have we found out anything new?' Danny said, following him into the room.

'I was just about to phone pathology to see if they've identified the bodies from the office building. Help yourself to tea or coffee, you look like you could do with a cup,' Edward said, leaving Danny as he headed for a desk with a phone.

Danny made himself a strong coffee and walked over to a line of portable whiteboards. They were full of blue-tacked pictures of Benton, Kristoff, Knowles and Mendes on one side, with arrows linking the stolen Pentic rifles to terrorist Abdel Belhadj and some Russian arms dealers, Nikolai and Ivan Korentski.

A set of pictures on one side caught his eye. They showed a dead night security guard, an office window with a circular hole cut in it, and a CCTV still of a figure on a motorbike. The image of the helmeted figure riding past them as they left the building site flashed through his mind. He was still studying it when Edward demanded everyone's attention.

'Ok, listen up everyone. Hush up,' he shouted, silencing the room. 'An hour ago a team of men posing as MI6 agents entered our secure pathology unit and removed all seven bodies from the mortuary along with their clothes, weapons and any items they carried. They presented MI6 identification and a signed order from myself to release the bodies. This, along with the rocket attack on Daniel Pearson's house, resulting in the deaths of Neil and Curtis, continues to indicate a serious criminal organisation that goes far beyond the skills and capabilities of any known terrorist cells we are monitoring. The clock is ticking, gentlemen. We have a missing pulse weapon planted in an as yet unknown destination, set for some time tomorrow,' said Edward, moving to the whiteboards. He tapped a grainy CCTV picture of the Transit with *ACM Event Management* signage.

'We have an entire department trawling through CCTV footage to find where this van went after leaving the industrial unit in Guildford. We urgently need to find the drivers, Peter Knowles and Miguel Mendes. Lastly, after finding the pulse weapon, the next priority is finding the only link we have to the organisation behind all of this, Commander Rex Benton,' said Edward banging on the photo of Benton.

'Well, you can forget Knowles and Mendes, they're dead. They were cleaning house when they came for me, Kristoff and Campbell. Benton doesn't make mistakes; he'll have killed them after the drop off,' said Danny from the back of the room.

All eyes in the room turned to look at him.

'Alright, considering the timeframe, we'll concentrate our efforts on tracking the van's movements, finding Benton and who gives him the orders,' said Edward, circling Benton with a marker.

'Shit. Orders. Hamish said he received his orders from a mysterious middle-aged toff, by encrypted emails. Where was Hamish living?' said Danny moving to the front next to Edward.

'They released Hamish Campbell on licence to his sister Alice's address in Stratford,' came Howard's voice from the coffee table.

'Let me take Scott and see if we can get the emails and find out who sent them,' said Danny suddenly full of energy and raring to go.

'No, we'll send a team and the techies,' said Edward dismissively.

'Aw, come on, Ed. Your guys aren't a patch on Scott and you know it. You said it yourself, time's of the essence,' said Danny pushing the point.

'Daniel has got a point,' said Howard chipping in.

Edward was silent for a moment as he thought about the options. Eventually he gave in.

'OK, get Scott and go. Tom, you go with them, and take it easy with Hamish's sister. Local plod have only just delivered the news that her brother's dead.'

Barely waiting for Edward's reply, Danny was already on the phone dialling Scott.

'Any sign of trouble, call it in,' Edward shouted after him.

Danny waved his hand in the air in acknowledgement as he walked towards the exit, closely followed by Tom. He tried to step around a nervous-looking Christopher Swash in his way, but the guy panicked, stepped in the same direction then stopped. Danny frowned at him. Swash physically shook, moving out of the way as fast as he could. Danny left, and the room went back to the murmuring hive of activity. With a trickle of nervous sweat running down the side of his face, Christopher Swash slipped unnoticed out of the door.

CHAPTER 45

Rufus had only been asleep for a few hours when his private line rang. He was awake and answering within two rings.

'Yes?'

'Sorry to bother you, General, we've had a message from Christopher Swash.'

'Mmm, what does that whining little idiot want?' grumbled Rufus, annoyed to be woken because of Swash.

'He says that Daniel Pearson is still alive and they're heading to Campbell's sister's address to decipher your encrypted emails to him,' he said, his voice tailing off towards the end of the message as he braced himself for Rufus's reaction.

'What? How the hell is Pearson still alive? Never mind. The emails are a military grade encryption, right? They assured me they can't be broken, correct?' Rufus bellowed, telling the nervous man rather than asking him.

'Eh, normally I would say yes, but apparently they have enlisted the help of world-renowned computer expert, Scott Miller.'

'Christ, I'm surrounded by idiots. Get the Commander and West, NOW! I'll be there in fifteen,' shouted Rufus, slamming the phone down without waiting for a response.

CHAPTER 46

Danny couldn't help smiling as Scott left his apartment and hurried to the car, with an excited grin on his face and a laptop bag slung over his shoulder.

'Good morning, chaps. Shall we catch some bad guys then?' Scott said, hopping in the back.

'Steady on, detective. I just need you to find a few emails,' said Danny with a chuckle.

'Ah yes, but they're encrypted emails, old boy. That's why a caveman like yourself needs computer genius like me,' Scott said with a little smugness.

'Ok, ok, we all agree you're the dog's bollocks. Now can we get on with this please?' said Danny, indicating for Tom to drive.

'A bit touchy today aren't we, and what's happened to your hair? One side looks like a Brillo pad.'

'Sorry, Scott, no sleep for two days and getting blown up tends to make me a little grumpy,' said Danny sarcastically as he tried to flatten his singed hair down.

'Apology accepted,' said Scott, missing the tone completely which put a smile on Danny's face.

'Right, where are we going, Tom?' said Danny turning back to the matter in hand.

'Stratford, 7 Gibbins Road, we'll be there soon. What's the plan?'

'We go in, flash the MI6 badge, you offer your deepest condolences—being the soft, caring type that you are—while Scott does his thing and I have a snoop through Hamish's stuff,' said Danny in an overly jovial tone, throwing a forced grin back Scott's way.

'Just like that,' Tom said.

'Yep, just like that.'

'Ok,' said Tom following the sat nav into the back end of Stratford.

They drove through the extreme mix of large modern glass and steel buildings built during and after the 2012 Olympics' regeneration of the area, and the old council-built houses and industrial units from decades long past. They turned into Gibbins Road, lined with square box 1960s terraced houses. Spying number seven, they pulled in behind a police patrol car and got out. Tom took the lead as he looked more believable as an MI6 agent than the more rugged and slightly dishevelled Danny. After knocking, the door opened and a five-foot-nothing, middle-aged family liaison officer stared back at them.

'Good afternoon, Officer...?' said Tom, flashing her his ID.

'Cole sir, Brenda Cole, family liaison,' she said looking past Tom at the frazzled-haired Danny and the floppy-haired, Armani-suited Scott.

'Well, Brenda, I'm Agent Trent and we need to ask Miss Campbell some questions regarding her brother.'

'Ok, let me just talk to her first,' she said turning back

into the house. She returned a minute later and indicated for them to follow.

Tom went in first, with Danny and Scott close behind. He followed Brenda into the small lounge where Alice Campbell looked up at them from the sofa. Bloodshot green eyes focused on them through a long mass of tight curly flame-red hair. Even in distress, Danny thought she was a stunning-looking woman.

'I'm sorry for your loss, Miss Campbell. I'm Agent Trent, MI6. These gentlemen are Agents Pearson and Miller. Now, we're sorry to disturb you so soon after your brother's death, but we have reason to believe there is information on your brother's computer that holds the key to who killed him. My colleagues here just need to see your brother's room,' said Tom, keeping his tone soft and sympathetic.

'I knew the stupid bastard was up to no good, all that sneaking off at all hours and different phones. I told him to keep his nose clean,' she blurted out, her eyes welling up again. 'Top of the stairs, the room on the right,' she said after a few seconds.

Danny and Scott left Tom and Brenda looking after her and went upstairs. Other than a makeshift computer desk made out of an old dressing table, Hamish's room was plain and sterile. It had a small wardrobe with just a handful of clothes, and a chest of drawers with underwear and a wash bag in. Scott sat at the dressing table and turned on the two different computers and laptop that adorned the top of it.

'Three computers, old boy, we could be here for a while.'

'Would it be easier to take them with us?' Danny said, looking back from the drawers.

'Mmm, let me have a go first. If I haven't got anywhere in an hour we'll take them back to headquarters.'

'Do your best, Scotty boy, time isn't something we have a lot of,' replied Danny pulling the drawers completely out to check underneath them. He grunted his frustration and slid the drawers back, then continued searching through the pockets of the clothes in the wardrobe.

'Come on, Hamish, you always had something to cover your arse tucked away somewhere,' he muttered to himself.

'Talking to yourself again, Daniel? First sign of madness, you know,' said Scott over his shoulder as he tapped furiously over three different keyboards.

Danny was about to answer when his hand caught something hard in a jacket pocket. When he pulled it out, it was a small silver key with the number 197 on it.

'Bingo,' he said, staring at the key.

'What is it?' said Scott, his interest piqued.

'Looks like a locker key,' Danny replied, still rooting through the wardrobe. When he didn't find anything else, he pulled out a sports bag from the bottom of the wardrobe. Placing it on the bed, Danny unzipped it and pulled out trainers, shorts and other gym kit. He was about to give up and throw it back in the wardrobe when he found a receipt for a protein drink in a side pocket. Unfolding it, the words *Gymbox, Chestnut Place, Westfield* revealed themselves. His mind ticked over as he held the key in one hand and the receipt in the other.

He's stashed something in a gym locker.

CHAPTER 47

Howard sat at the back of the MI6 incident room. He'd been sitting there for quite some time taking in all the boards and information as he thought through the possible suspects. Eventually Edward wandered over to him.

'Penny for your thoughts,' he said, pulling out a chair and sitting next to him.

'I'm not sure you'd like the answer,' Howard replied, uncharacteristically serious.

'Try me.'

'The way I see it there are three scenarios. One, Abdel Belhadj, or one of his splinter cells, is getting help from a highly organised group or a government—the Russians or Chinese perhaps. Or two, this is all orchestrated by another country for reasons we don't yet know.' Howard paused momentarily, a frown crossing his forehead.

'And three,' said Edward, prompting him to continue.

'Three, dear boy, is that one of our own agencies is working to their own agenda,' Howard said getting up from his seat. 'Excuse me, Edward, I need to make a phone call.'

'Yes, of course,' Edward said, watching him go. Turning his attention back to the front, he caught Christopher Swash watching him from the other side of the room. When he realised Edward had spotted him, he nervously darted his head round and did a poor job of trying to look engrossed in his computer screen. Edward logged it in his mind as strange, then turned his attention back to the whiteboards at the front of the room.

Out in the corridor Howard checked he was alone before making a call.

'Howard, what an unexpected pleasure.'

'Good afternoon, Rufus. I'll get straight to the point. I'm sure you have heard all about the excitement in the capital last night.'

'Of course. I wouldn't run much of a counter-terrorist organisation if I hadn't, would I? said the General with an air of arrogance.

'Quite. Due to the shortlist of suspects with the capability of such a well-equipped and organised attack, I think we should meet. After all, this is as embarrassing to Project Dragonfly as it is to Secret Services,' said Howard, leaving the words hanging in the air to see what Rufus's reaction would be.

'Mmm, I'm inclined to agree,' the General finally said. 'I'm having an emergency meeting with the PM and Pringle straight after their press meeting at Central Hall tomorrow, why don't you join us there?' he continued after a pause.

'Thank you, Rufus, I will see you then.'

'Good. After all, we're all on the same side, aren't we, old chap?' said Rufus hanging up without waiting for an answer.

'On the same side. Mmm, I'm not so sure about that,' Howard murmured to himself. He paced the corridor thinking for a minute or two, then made another call.

'What do you want, Howard?' came Danny's gruff voice.

'Careful with the sentiment, Daniel, people will think you care,' said Howard with deadpan humour.

'I'll say it again, what do you want, Howard?' came Danny's response, as gruff as the first one.

'Has Scott uncovered anything yet?'

'Hang on,' Danny said.

The phone went quiet. Seconds later Scott's dulcet tones came over.

'Howard, old man, how can I help?'

'Have you found anything at Campbell's?'

'I'm afraid not. The two PCs contain nothing of interest and the encryption on the laptop is going to take some time to crack.'

'Ok, get the laptop and yourselves back to headquarters, you might as well work on it here.'

'Right you are. Oh, Daniel wants to talk to you,' said Scott, handing the phone back to Danny.

'Listen, I've found a locker key and a gym receipt in Hamish's things. I think the slippery bastard's stashed something in his gym locker,' Danny said.

'Ok, send Scott back with Tom. You go and follow your lead, see where it goes,' said Howard, pausing the conversation when Christopher Swash shuffled out of the incident room and passed him slowly on his way to the toilets.

'Roger that,' was all Danny said in response, then hung up.

Howard slid the phone into his pocket, his eyes never leaving the toilet door. Eventually he turned, walked back into the incident room and headed for the coffee machine.

He caught the attention of Edward, who wandered casually over to him.

'Any news?' he said, grabbing a cup and joining Howard.

'Not at Campbell's. Tom's bringing Scott back with a laptop that needs cracking, and Daniel's gone to the gym.'

'Eh, what? This is no time for a workout,' said Edward, his face full of surprise.

'No, he's found a locker key at Campbell's and thinks he may have hidden something there,' said Howard with an uncharacteristic smile on his face.

'Mmm, not much to go on. We've got to turn this around, time's running out.'

'Quite. I've got an emergency meeting with the PM, the Minister for Defence and General McManus at Central Hall tomorrow morning. I would very much like to tell him we've found the missing pulse weapon and have a suspect in custody. We're missing something, Edward, the answer is staring us in the face and we're miss— Who is that?' said Howard, his eyes following Christopher Swash as he shuffled back into the room and scooted back to his desk.

'Christopher Swash, data analyst. Odd chap,' said Edward curiously. 'Why?'

'If I were a suspicious man, I'd swear he was spying on me.'

'Howard, you are a suspicious man,' Edward answered back.

'Yes I am, Edward. Do me a favour, keep an eye on that one.'

CHAPTER 48

'll see you two back at HQ,' Danny said waving Tom and Scott off from Campbell's front door.

He moved back inside and stepped past Brenda, the liaison officer, to talk to Alice.

'Miss Campbell, did your brother use a gym called Gymbox?' said Danny as gently as he could.

'Eh, yes, we both did, it's in the Westfield Centre, just across the footbridge on Jupp Road,' she said looking up at him with piercing green eyes as she brushed her long, curly red hair back and pointed towards the back of the estate.

'Eh, sorry. Did you ever use a locker?' stammered Danny, unnerved by her looks. She seemed to sense his interest and gave him a shy smile.

'No, but Hamish did. You get one with the gold membership; I only have silver, so I didn't have one.'

'Ok, thank you very much. I'll leave you with Brenda,' said Danny, turning.

A movement across the road caught his eye out of the living room window. Brenda was saying something behind him as he watched two figures tucking in on the corner of the house opposite. They were dressed like armed police, but Danny was sure they weren't. He darted his head to the other end of the terraced block to see two more on that corner, MP5 semi-automatic carbine rifles raised, and their caps pulled low to their shades so he couldn't see their faces clearly. His senses tingling, Danny had the strong feeling Benton and West were out there. Lifting his shirt at the back, he pulled his Glock 17 out of its belt holster.

'We've gotta go, now,' he said to the shocked women.

'What are you doing, what's up?' stammered Brenda turning and walking over to the window.

'No, don't go near—'

Silenced rounds pinged and popped through the glass hitting Brenda in the chest, knocking her off her feet as if pulled by an invisible rope. She was dead before she hit the carpet.

'Out the back now,' shouted Danny, grabbing Alice's arm and dragging her shrieking out of the living room.

Heading to the back door, Danny saw a dark shadow through its frosted glass. As it turned, the blurred shape of a rifle was clear to see. Without hesitation Danny put three bullets through the glass, striking the shadow centre of the head. He pulled the door open as the body fell towards him. Seeing a second gunman to his left, he caught the dead man, spinning him towards his partner as he opened fire. The body shook with the impact, the body armour stopping the bullets going right through the body into Danny.

Swinging his gun arm up under the man's armpit, Danny peered over his shoulder to aim and put a bullet through the second guy's forehead. Letting his man drop, Danny reached in and grabbed Alice's wrist, dragging her shocked and shaking body out the door.

'How do we get out of here? Where is the footbridge?'

Danny said firmly, making sure he had eye contact to drive the question home.

'Oh my God, oh my God. Eh, through the gate and left across Jupp Road,' she said, flustered.

Pulling her so her feet nearly left the floor, Danny hurtled towards the garden gate. Opening it, he darted his head through to grab a quick sweep of the alley, the sound of the front door being broken in behind forcing him on. The alleyway was clear, so he headed left, still gripping Alice tight.

'Ow, you're hurting me,' she shouted, shocking him to a stop.

'I'm sorry. Look, we need to get somewhere public, lots of people. Ok?' Danny said, fighting to sound soft and patient while he looked around for armed killers.

'Who are they? Why are they shooting at you?' she said, confused.

'Us, Alice. They killed your brother and they want to kill us in case he told us anything. I'll explain everything later. Now we need to go,' Danny said looking directly at her. Her features changed as the animal will to survive kicked in and her inner strength grew.

'Ok,' she said with a nod.

'Good, stick close behind me and do exactly as I say. Let's go.'

With that, Danny moved down the alley walking fast, almost at a jog. Swinging his head behind him, he expected to see a gunman coming out the garden gate at any second. He slowed, ready to take a darting look out of the alley into Jupp Road. Two feet from the opening, the barrel of a rifle followed by another gunman in fake police kit appeared. Danny hit the rifle to one side with his gun hand as the man squeezed the trigger, sending a suppressed round whizzing past his ear. Driving forward with all his power and body weight behind him, Danny punched him square in the Adam's apple, crushing his windpipe. He went down, dropping everything to clamp his gloved hands around his neck in a futile effort to make his airway open back up.

Danny bobbed down and took the man's Glock out of his holster, sliding it in the holster on his belt. He scanned Jupp Road but couldn't see any more of them. Turning back, Danny beckoned Alice towards him. As she moved, he spotted a figure behind her darting his head out the garden gate. Locking his arm straight, Danny let a couple of rounds off to keep their heads down while they made off across the road. They ran up and over the metal footbridge with the railway tracks below that ran to and from Stratford station. The entrance to Westfield Shopping Centre lay just beyond the station, fifty metres away. Glancing behind him before they descended the ramp on the far side, Danny could see two men following while the others pulled the bodies into vans, slammed the doors and screamed off out of the estate.

They'll drive round and try to cut us off in a kill box.

'We've gotta move,' Danny said tucking the handgun into the back of his jeans next to the holstered one, pulling his shirt over them. Danny broke into a run, as they neared the station he checked Alice was behind him, pleased to see her easily keeping up. She was lithe and athletic and obviously one of the ones that actually used their gym membership. They ran around the bus terminal and passed the train station entrance. He slowed as they started up the steps, blending in with the flow of shoppers as they headed to the entrance of Westfield Shopping Centre. Danny looked back to the footbridge they'd just crossed. One of the vans pulled up and the two men who'd followed them over got in the back. Swinging his head the other way

Danny spotted the other van. Its doors opened and three men got out. They'd lost the body armour, hats and rifles in favour of light jackets and shades. Even from that distance Danny's trained eye could spot the holstered handguns. Reaching the top of the steps, he turned to the first van again and saw the same story: two guys getting out, jackets and shades. Benton and West.

'Let's go,' he said to Alice.

They turned and walked calmly towards the entrance to the Centre like any other shoppers. Alice moved up beside him and unexpectedly gripped his hand as she walked glued to his side. He smiled at her to reassure her, hiding his senses on high alert and the adrenaline surging through his body. Passing through the entrance, Danny steered them to the information desk and picked up a plan of the Centre.

CHAPTER 49

Rufus snatched the headset tentatively offered by one of his minions. Placing it on his head he ran his eyes through the hijacked camera feeds surrounding Stratford's modern shopping centre.

'Commander, talk to me, what the hell is going on?' he demanded.

Static followed by some wind noise and breathing crackled its way over the speakers before the Commander's breathless voice made its way through.

'Pearson's got away with Campbell's sister, they're on foot and have just entered Westfield Shopping Centre. We are in pursuit,' said Benton, obviously on the move.

'I am not in the habit of repeating myself, Commander, so I will say this one last time. Kill Pearson and get anything he got from Campbell's,' said the General, a little calmer.

'And the girl?'

'Kill her.'

'Yes sir,' said Benton without hesitation.

'And, Commander, do it quickly. Project Dragonfly

cannot intervene and close security on a public place of
that size. There would be too many questions and an
inquiry. You're on your own.'

'Yes, General,' came Benton's unemotional response.

Rufus turned his back to the screens, pulled off the
headset thrusting it back to the man, making him jump.
Making his way to the back of the room and out of earshot
he made another call. It answered on the second ring.

'Yes.'

'Pearson and Campbell's sister got away. The
Commander has become a liability. Proceed as planned,
and Hawk, make sure you retrieve any information they
got from Hamish Campbell. Is that clear?'

'Crystal, General. Location?' The Hawk said with no
discernible accent or emotion.

'They're in Stratford, Westfield Shopping Centre.'

'I'll be there in seven minutes,' finished The Hawk, the
screaming of his motorcycle engine drowning out all other
sounds before he hung up.

The General stood for a moment, his mind racing,
evaluating and re-evaluating the mission. He still rated his
chances of success as high.

*Howard, the Prime Minister and that idiot Pringle will be taken out
by the pulse weapon tomorrow. The blame will be squarely placed on
Jarrel Belhadj. Once Pearson is taken care of and Commander
Benton is retired, I'll send The Hawk to take care of the last loose
end, that snivelling idiot Swash.*

Spurred on by his own mental pep talk, Rufus marched to
the front of the room and clicked his fingers to the headset
guy, who jumped back into action and handed them over.

198

'Status report please, Commander.'

'Myself and West have entered the Centre by the main entrance. Fisher and Martel are proceeding to the entrance by the Holiday Inn hotel, while Butler takes the far entrance by John Lewis.'

'Excellent, we are patching into the Centre's CCTV system now. I will update you once I have a positive ID and location,' said Rufus, growing in confidence all the time.

'Roger that, standing by for guidance.'

CHAPTER 50

fter a quick study of the Centre's plan, Danny took Alice's hand and walked relaxed and confidently through the shops and shoppers as any couple would. His confidence rubbed off a little on Alice, who hung on his arm as they moved. He would have liked the Centre to be heaving with people, so they could disappear into the crowd but it was only half full, it still offered enough shoppers for him to know that Benton's men wouldn't open fire in the public areas. The main walkway ran past all the shops in a long sweeping curve with a floor below and a floor above. Just before they'd travelled too far along the walkway for its shape to cut off the view back to the entrance doors, Danny tucked Alice into the entrance to Skechers and craned his head back. His eyes flicked and scanned in millisecond movements, from face to face as he trusted his senses to pick out any of the gunmen. He spotted them in no time, Benton and West. They were standing stock still scanning the crowd, faces void of emotion, calculating. Benton put his hand to his earpiece to listen, then as if drawn by magnetism, looked straight at Danny.

'Let's go,' he said to Alice, gently pulling her back into the crowds and away from Benton. Danny had his eyes fixed on the halfway point around the curve, where a walkway teed-off to the left, leading to an exit to the Holiday Inn hotel, eateries and the entrance to the Olympic Park. It was also the direction of Gymbox and Hamish's locker. A quick glance behind him confirmed Benton and West following fifty metres behind. Reaching the intersection of walkways, Danny turned to head towards Gymbox. Before he could get more than two feet, he spotted Fisher and Martel coming through the entrance ahead of them. Fisher's mouth moved as he communicated with the voice over the earpiece; as with Benton, his eyes found Danny all too quickly. Swinging Alice around, he turned back. A look to his right confirmed Benton closing in and with a look to the left, he picked Butler's regimented movements out as he approached from the far entrance. Danny didn't look back behind him. He knew Fisher and Martel were closing. Looking up at the black-domed 360-degree CCTV cameras answered Danny's fears.

They're patched into the Centre's CCTV. But they won't have the individual stores' cameras.'

Without hesitation Danny led Alice into Primark department store. He weaved his way through the rows of men's and women's clothes, bags and shoes. At the seating area in the shoe section Danny spun Alice around and sat her down.

Leaning in, he whispered in her ear, 'Stay here, I'll be back in a minute.'

When she clutched his arm, her eyes wide in panic, Danny smiled at her and leaned in again. 'It's ok, I'm going to even up the odds. I'll be back, I promise.'

She reluctantly let him go. He winked at her and turned away. Walking slightly stooped, Danny kept his eye line just above the racks of clothes as he located Fisher, Martel and Butler entering the shop. They spread out as they moved further into the store in a predictable sweep formation. Benton and West didn't enter the shop. Danny wasn't surprised, they would probably go down and enter the shop via the lower ground entrance. Passing a rack of baseball caps and sun hats, Danny picked a baseball cap and slid it on his head, pulling it down low. From their view, they wouldn't see enough to identify him. Looking at the rack the hats hung from, Danny dumped a row of them on the floor and unhooked the foot-long notched steel rod, off its slot in the shelving wall behind. He put the flat piece in the palm of his hand and closed it into a fist, with the grooved rod sticking straight out between his middle fingers in a makeshift blade.

Heading towards Fisher on the far left, Danny sunk below the top of the clothes racks like a predatory shark going below the water's surface. As Fisher got within ten feet, Danny backed in between a row of coats, disappearing to the back. When he saw Fisher through his narrow slice of view, Danny launched himself forward, punching the metal rod into Fisher's inner thigh. Gripped firmly in his fist, the rod tore its way into the flesh, severing Fisher's femoral artery. Pulling the rod out unleashed an unstoppable river of blood. Looking down in surprise, fear and confusion, Fisher gripped the wound in panic. Danny dropped the racking rod and grabbed the weakening Fisher's top, pulling him in between the coats. Clamping a hand over his mouth, Danny held Fisher tight. He struggled a little, but the blood loss was so fast his blood pressure dropped like a stone and he passed out. Leaving Fisher in the middle of the coats, Danny stood back and dragged the whole clothes stand towards him just far enough to hide the pooling blood.

He took a quick look over the top of the display and targeted Butler on the far side by the changing rooms. Taking a wide arc past the entrance, Danny kept one eye on Martel's back and the other on Butler who'd gone into the changing rooms. Picking up a couple of hideous flowery shirts Danny slid into the changing rooms holding them up to hide his face.

'Excuse me, mate, is it ok to try these on?' Danny said in his best impatient customer impression.

Butler backed out of a cubicle and turned unalarmed. Throwing the shirts forward over Butler's head, Danny powered his fist into Butler's face, shattering his nose through the garments and knocking him back into a cubicle. As Butler landed on his back, Danny took a run up and kicked him in the balls with all his might, sliding him across the laminate flooring until he hit the mirror. Pulling the gun out of his jeans, Danny used the hard metal casing to repeatedly whack Butler over the head until he stopped moving. Pulling the shirts off him, Danny backed out closing the cubicle door behind him. Digging in his pocket for a coin he slotted it in the groove on the outside of the lock and turned it to secure the cubicle. A shop attendant had returned to the front of the changing rooms as he was leaving. He gave her one of his best smiles, reading her name badge as he approached.

'Any good?' she said, returning the smile.

'I have my moments, Sandra. But I'm afraid the shirts didn't fit,' Danny said, making her blush as he handed her the clothes.

Back on the shop floor he spotted Martel getting near the shoes and Alice. Moving as fast as he could without running, Danny weaved between the racks. As he got close to Martel, a scream echoed through the store as a customer came across Fisher's blood-soaked body. Everyone including Martel turned to stare in the direction of the noise. Using the distraction, Danny got close enough to grab Martel around the neck before he discovered Alice sitting in front of him. In a twist of monumental power he snapped Martel's neck, rendering him lifeless in his arms. Sliding him onto the seating, Danny propped him up against a shoe rack and left him there. Alice had a hand to her mouth and was looking up at Danny, shaking.

'It's ok, I won't let anything happen to you. Now we've got to get out of here,' he said holding out his hand.

Shakily, she took it and moved with Danny as he headed for the escalators. While the commotion grew around Fisher's body, Danny and Alice slid silently out of sight on the escalator to the floor below.

CHAPTER 51

anny spotted Benton and West easily at the lower level entrance to the store. He turned his back to them and tipped his head down to block the view of Alice as they descended the last few feet to the bottom of the escalator. Looking up at him, Alice slid her hand up the side of his face. Ignoring Danny's confusion at her move, she continued up and pulled the label off his stolen baseball cap. Holding it up in front of him she smiled sweetly, her emerald green eyes locking on his. Danny fought off the attraction he had for her, now was not the time.

'There's going to be a rush, so stay close and follow my lead,' he said, glad to see Alice keeping it together as she nodded back.

They stepped off the escalator and Alice followed Danny around the side to a point where a pillar, the clothes racks and the side of the escalator obscured the view of them from shoppers, cameras or the entrance.

'Get ready,' Danny said. He pulled out the Glock taken from the man in Judd Road and unloaded the entire clip into the wall opposite, dropping the empty weapon when he'd finished.

The effect was instantaneous. After the deafening gunshots, shoppers dropped everything and ran. Families grabbed their kids, and screams and shouts echoed through the store. Danny moved out from behind the pillar with Alice in tow.

'Get out, NOW. There's a guy back there with a gun. Get out, get out,' Danny shouted at the top of his voice.

Putting his hand out behind him, he felt the reassuring grip of Alice's hand in his. Firmly linked, he squeezed into the middle of the panicking bottleneck and forced their way out of the entrance to the store and into the lower ground walkway. Danny couldn't see Benton; he would have been forced way back or may have aborted the mission.

The Centre would be crawling with armed police within ten minutes. Danny got a lock on West not far in front of him, he was trying to fight his way through the crowds towards the escalators and the exit. Pushing forwards, Danny split the shoppers apart and launched at West, taking him fully by surprise. Grabbing his jacket, Danny hammered his forehead into the bridge of West's nose, crunching bone and cartilage as it caved in and poured with blood. As West went down, Danny rained a blistering combination of punches to his body and head. He hit the floor hard, stunned and dazed as Danny unzipped his jacket to expose his gun.

'Quick, help me hold him down, he's the gunman,' Danny yelled at the top of his voice. Most gave him a wide berth, afraid to get involved, but as the seconds ticked by two guys and a Centre security guard grabbed West and knelt on him, pinning him to the spot.

As quickly as he'd moved on West, Danny backed into

the crowd. He grabbed Alice's hand and led her away up the escalator. Within seconds they'd turned down the walkway and exited by the Holiday Inn. Danny's eyes moved through the crowd darting from left to right looking for Benton or his men. When neither presented themselves, he led Alice on towards the gym.

Sirens sounded in the air, causing the customers in cafes and eateries to look back at the panicking hordes of shoppers leaving the Centre. Away from the chaos, Danny had a last look around before following Alice into the gym. Fixing his best friendly smile on his face, Danny moved towards the reception ready to blag his way in. Alice moved in front of him before he got there and grinned at the young muscular guy on the desk.

'Hi Reese. I left my purse in my brother's locker and it's got my gym pass in it. Can you buzz me through so I can get it, please?' she said sweetly with wide innocent eyes.

'Yeah, go through,' said Reese, obviously fancying her as he couldn't buzz them through the barrier quick enough.

Danny followed her down a corridor to a row of lockers outside the changing rooms. With the key in his hand, he followed the numbers as they ran up to the 197 written on the key.

'Here's the moment of truth,' he said sliding the key into the lock. It turned, and the locker popped open. After a quick look both ways Danny reached in and pulled out a small black rucksack. He unzipped it and found a manila folder and half a dozen memory sticks. Taking the folder out, Danny opened it and took a quick look. It was full of photos and photocopied email correspondence and copies of flight tickets and passports. Flicking further, he found the fake ACM Event Management ID for Knowles and Mendes, and a works order for a delivery to Central Hall,

Westminster. With the penny dropping, Danny closed it and zipped it away in the rucksack. He hung it off his back by one strap and closed the locker.

'Let's get you somewhere safe,' he said to Alice.

'Where's that?' Alice replied with a worried look.

'I've got to get this back to MI6 headquarters straight away and we'll sort everything else out from there, ok?'

She nodded and followed Danny out of the gym. He ignored the crowds and police at the shopping centre behind them, as they sealed the area off for an armed response unit to deal with the bodies in Primark, arresting West and the semi-conscious Butler ready to whisk them away for questioning. Walking the other way, Danny and Alice turned down Westfield Avenue and hailed the first taxi that went by.

CHAPTER 52

Scott and Tom arrived at MI6 headquarters. They cleared security and headed up in the lift to the incident room. Scott was pointed in the direction of Edward's excited young techies, thrilled at the chance to work with Scott Miller, the world renowned computer expert. Scott, in return, lapped up the attention.

'Good afternoon, gentlemen, may I have some desk space, a couple of monitors and a keyboard and mouse please?' he said grinning as he brushed his floppy sand-coloured hair out of his eyes. The techies immediately moved out of their chairs and fulfilled Scott's requests.

'Top form. How would you chaps like to learn how to break a 128-bit encrypted security password in under twenty minutes?'

Placing Hamish's laptop on the table, Scott connected his own and various keyboards and monitors. He barely had time to get started when phones started ringing all around the room. Before Howard and Edward could find out what was going on, both their mobiles rang. Scott looked around as phones went down and up, and people started moving in and out of the room with purpose.

'I say, Edward, old man. What's going on?' Scott said, tapping Edward on the arm.

'There are reports of shooting at Campbell's address, and gunfire in Westfield Shopping Centre. Sorry, Scott, I've got to go,' said Edward dismissing Scott and heading over to Howard.

'Listen up, people, armed response are en route. I want three teams of agents down there, like, yesterday. Come on, go, go,' Edward yelled into the room.

'Any news of Daniel or Miss Campbell?' Howard said to Edward.

'No, early reports say there's at least two dead bodies in the shopping centre. No positive IDs as yet.'

'Mmm, you get down there, Edward. I'll stay here and see if they get a trace on the missing ACM Transit van, and find out what Mr Miller can do with Hamish's laptop. After all, time is running out and we still have a missing lethal weapon planned for detonation tomorrow,' said Howard light-heartedly as if he was discussing plans for lunch.

Edward's face dropped as the reminder forced the gravity of the situation to the front of his mind.

As they stood there Christopher Swash walked past, his coat on as he was leaving for the night. He noticed Howard and Edward looking at him and nervously said goodnight.

'Goodnight,' Edward said back as Christopher disappeared out of the door.

'Did you find anything on our friend there?' Howard said.

'Yes, it would seem he's a little too familiar with the bookies,' Edward said with raised eyebrows.

'How familiar?'

'About twenty thousand pounds' worth of familiar,' Edward said dryly.

'Mmm, a perfect target for manipulation. Let's have a little chat with Mr Swash in the morning.'

'Ok, I'm off to Stratford. I'll keep you informed,' said Edward heading out the door.

CHAPTER 53

Benton exited the Centre as soon as he heard gunfire and saw the crowds of shoppers approaching. He was across the pedestrian bridge and down the steps by Stratford train station as the police sirens sounded their impending arrival. One of the vans had already evacuated the area while the other one hung on, nervously waiting for any of the team to get out before the police arrived. Hanging out of the window, the driver spotted Benton and waved him over.

'Hurry, we've gotta get out of here,' he said urgently as Benton hopped in the passenger seat.

The second the door shut, the van was away. Benton could feel an uneasiness in the van. The driver and Tillman in the back looked tense, shifting in their seats.

'The General wants us back to base,' the driver finally said.

Benton's hand twitched and he fought the images of the cellar triggered by the atmosphere and confines of the van. He'd failed to kill Pearson and get any information Hamish had hidden away. The General had ordered his termination. He could feel it. They'd drive him somewhere quiet and execute him. Moving his eyes but not his head, he flicked to the wing mirror. The second van had pulled into line behind them, the General's idea of backup. The phantom smell filled his nostrils, the burning rancid ammonia of his own piss and shit. He moved his eyes to the mirror in the centre of the windscreen. The image of one of his ISIS tormentors took Tillman's place. Benton had to squeeze his eyes shut to chase it away. Opening them, he saw Tillman looking at the back of his head, his hand inside his jacket on the grip of his gun.

The van headed into a rundown industrial area, the setup for the kill. With no alarming movements, Benton had his arm around his waist gripping his own gun. He subtly adjusted the angle back behind him and squeezed off three shots. They exited out of the back of the seat, catching Tillman in the middle of his chest. Benton had his gun at the driver's temple before Tillman slumped to the van floor. The driver opened his mouth to say something, but Benton wasn't interested in anything he had to say and pulled the trigger. The bullet passed through the drivers head, blowing a huge lump out of the other side as it exited, shattering the driver's side window. Reaching down, Benton yanked the handbrake up and braced as the van's rear wheels locked up, snaking it to a halt. Hopping in the back, he picked up one of the team's MP5 semi-automatic carbine rifles and ran for the back doors. He kicked the release handle, sending the doors flying open as he jumped out. The last thing the team in the van behind saw was Benton bursting out of the rear doors with his rifle up and levelled before he emptied an entire magazine into their van.

Benton stood for a second, rifle still up, smoke whispering out of its muzzle. The release from the confined van

213

to the fresh air flashed images of his escape from the cellar into the bright Afghanistan sunshine. Dropping the weapon, Benton squeezed his eyes shut and clenched his shaking hand into a fist until the images went away.

'Pearson,' he said to himself through gritted teeth. Composing himself, he turned and shut the van doors then walked to the driver's door. Opening it, he pulled the driver's body out onto the ground and hopped in. Starting it up he drove calmly off, turning back out of the industrial area and onto the main road, sticking to the speed limit as he went.

CHAPTER 54

The further the taxi got from the shopping centre, the more Danny's adrenaline levels dropped. The intense concentration and physical effort of combat thrived on adrenaline, but once that was gone, relief and fatigue set in fast. He was suddenly aware that Alice held his arm tightly, with her long, curly mop of red hair resting on his shoulder.

'Are you alright?' he said softly.

'I think so,' she replied in a low voice followed by a long pause. 'Thank you,' she finally said.

'What for?' Danny replied, puzzled.

'Saving my life,' she said, a tear trickling down her cheek.

'Oh, eh, right,' Danny replied, embarrassed by the sentiment but strangely glad of the closeness.

They drove on towards central London. An array of different response vehicles screamed past them on their way towards Westfield Shopping Centre, thinning out to nothing the further away they got.

'Jesus, what's this bloody clown doin',' came the thick

cockney tone of the taxi driver's voice. Up ahead, a lorry had swerved to avoid a turning car and crashed into the pedestrian crossing lights, blocking the road as other drivers honked horns and shouted out their car windows.

'Hold tight, I'll cut down Montague Street and get around them,' he said hammering on his horn, forcing the car in front to move up so he could turn across the road and off down his diversion.

Thankfully the road was clear and quiet. They drove along the tree-lined suburban road, slowing for the speed bumps periodically placed as they went. The taxi driver had just gone over one by a road on his right, when a red Royal Mail truck hurtled out at them. It hit them squarely in the side without braking. The impact knocked the driver out and blew the windows in as it pushed the car sideways off the road and across the pavement. It crunched them to a halt, wedging them firmly against a wall on one side and the front of the truck on the other.

Trying to shake the ringing in his ears, Danny pushed a shrieking Alice off him so he could get to the gun in its holster behind him. The truck driver's door opened and the crash helmeted image of The Hawk appeared at the front of the taxi between the bonnet and truck front. Danny managed to get his fingers on the Glock's grip when The Hawk pointed a thin gas-powered gun at his chest. He pumped the trigger twice, moved it a couple of inches and pumped the trigger again. Danny felt two sharp jabs in his chest and was aware that Alice had abruptly stopped screaming. Pulling his gun out of its holster he brought it in front of him. His head was swimming and, try as he might, the Glock seemed to have turned into an immovable object of enormous weight. Gritting his teeth, Danny tried again. His vision blurred and his body slumped as he lost consciousness.

CHAPTER 55

Parking the van on a quiet suburban road a mile from his house in Hounslow, Benton sat back and waited an hour until the sun went down. He took a walk he knew well, through the housing estates and linking alleys to come out on a road that ran parallel to the one his house was on. Walking along until he reached the house that backed on to his own, Benton took a casual look around for observers. No one was in sight. He walked confidently through the gate on the side of the house and headed into their back garden. The light was on in the kitchen, but with the garden in darkness Benton doubted anyone inside could see much past the kitchen light reflecting back in their own window.

With a little run-up and the lightest of pulls, Benton vaulted silently over the six-foot fence, dropping to a squat facing the back of his house. He stayed there motionless, hidden in the shadows, watching and listening. Tactically this was a stupid move, but Benton needed his go bag with its money, fake passports, clothes and various other IDs. He was about to move when the smell and images of him hanging in the Afghanistan cellar flashed to the front of his mind. Benton bit hard into his forearm, the pain chasing the images away as he drew blood. He'd hidden his worsening post-traumatic stress psychosis from everyone. The General would have drummed him out of Project Dragonfly if he'd known. But now he was out, Benton had to face the fact that the problem was out of control and he had to get some help.

Focused back on the dark house, he moved up to the back door and crouched down. Flicking his phone light on, Benton checked the bottom of the door. Frowning, he shone the light on the floor and picked up the little rubber wedge he always slid in the gap at the bottom of the door, to check if anyone had entered while he was away. Swiftly turning the light off, he gently placed his ear on the door and listened. Nothing, not a sound. Sliding across the back wall, Benton craned his head round and looked in through the kitchen window. Nothing, all dark and quiet. He slid a commando knife out of its sheath on his belt and slid it forcefully into the seal of the closed window. Wiggling the razor sharp blade, he pushed it through to the inside and teased the locking handle up, popping the window open. Freezing like a statue, Benton stood listening again. Satisfied, he hopped up and climbed onto the sink before lowering himself silently onto the kitchen floor. Flicking the phone light on again, he shone it on the inside of the back door. A lump of plastic explosive with a mercury trigger switch looked back at him. His hand trembled a little as he turned the light off again. He moved cautiously into the hall and checked the front door to find more plastic. Ignoring it, he continued up the stairs and slid stealthily into his bedroom. Standing well back in the dark shadows, Benton scanned the road outside. He picked out the blue panel van parked a little way up the road. As he watched, a little red dot of a cigarette being sucked appeared in the front. A second later a puff of smoke drifted out the open side window. A little smile twitched in the corner of his mouth.

Amateurs.

Keeping to the middle of the room, Benton headed for the mirror on the wall. He slid his hand up the side and pushed a little catch. The mirror was hinged on one side and swung into the room to expose a large wall safe. Opening it, Benton grabbed his go bag, some more cash and a stack of burner phones. Putting them all in the bag, he snapped his old phone in two and chucked it in the safe. He didn't bother closing it. No point. He'd never be coming back here.

Making his way back down to the kitchen, he was about to climb back out the window when he stopped and moved to the door. Disconnecting the detonator from the plastic explosive and the mercury trigger, Benton removed the device and left out the door. After re-negotiating the fence, he made a minor diversion before taking the mile walk to his stolen van. Starting it up, he drove purposely toward his house, slowing as he passed the blue panel van to give them a sideways look before accelerating away. Watching in the mirrors, Benton saw the van lights go on as they started up. The van lurched forward in pursuit, before opening up like a tin can in a huge ball of fire as it triggered the mercury switch on the lump of plastic explosive Benton had sneaked under its rear on his way out. As he disappeared into the night, Benton ran through his options.

Call up my contacts and be out of the country by the morning, that's what I should do. But I have a debt to settle first.

CHAPTER 56

The General's large black Range Rover moved silently in through the open doorway to the derelict warehouse. It splashed through the puddles and weaved around the concrete support pillars before turning to a stop in the centre, facing back towards the doorway. It sat there waiting, the bright xenon headlights casting ominous shadows through the wafting exhaust fumes. Without warning, the sound of a powerful motorbike engine echoed off the walls, and a single headlight tore through the darkness for the far corner of the warehouse. It moved along the side of the building before circling to a stop by the Range Rover's blacked-out rear window.

Looking over, The Hawk stared through his own concealing black visor and waited patiently. The car window slid smoothly down until Rufus's face came into view. The Hawk clicked his visor up just far enough to talk but not far enough to expose any more than his mouth.

'Good evening, Mr Hawk. You have something for me?' said Rufus in a more jovial mood than usual.

The Hawk pulled the zip down on his Kevlar motorcycle jacket and pulled the file from Hamish's locker out. He handed it over and zipped the jacket back up.

'Splendid, and Pearson and the girl?' said Rufus, his eyes sharpening as he stared at the helmet visor, trying to glimpse the man inside.

'Terminated,' The Hawk said bluntly.

'Excellent. Payment will be in your account within the hour. I have another job if you are interested. Commander Benton has become a liability and is proving a little difficult to retire.'

'London is too hot right now and my services are required overseas. I'm afraid I will have to decline this time,' The Hawk replied, his voice neutral and emotionless, hiding his Serbian nationality.

'Fair enough, don't be a stranger. I can always use a man with your talents,' said Rufus facing forward without waiting for a response as he pressed the button to put the window up.

The Hawk clicked his crash helmet down and pulled away in front of the Range Rover. He left the warehouse just ahead of the General's car and opened the bike up, screaming away into the distance before the car had left the opening.

CHAPTER 57

G roggy, Danny could sense movement before he could open his eyes, a gentle rhythmic vibration, low and comforting. With his head full of cotton wool, he forced his eyes to open, expecting relief from the darkness and an answer to the question of where he was. All he got was confusion as the pitch black was met by more pitch black.

With his senses and focus kicking back in, Danny felt around him. He was on something large and soft and wrapped in plastic. Moving his hand further across, he recoiled sharply at the touch of something warm and soft. A murmur followed which led him to the conclusion it was Alice. Feeling around the edge of what they were lying on, he decided it must be a mattress. There was a jerk, a vibration and a pull to one side, causing him to roll into Alice. She mumbled a semi-conscious response and swung her arm over him, holding him tight.

Firing on all cylinders, Danny figured they were in the back of a lorry. Without pulling away he felt through his pockets. His gun was gone, which he wasn't surprised about, but he did find his phone inside his jacket pocket. He pulled it out and fumbled for the button on the side to turn it on. It burst into light, hurting his eyes in the darkness. Once it finished booting up he tapped the light on and illuminated the inside of a metal shipping container. Spinning the light around, Danny could see that they were on a stack of brand new mattresses surrounded by dozens and dozens of more new mattresses. He turned the light to see Alice. Her long, curly red hair hid half her face as she nuzzled into his neck. He reached across gently and moved it back to expose her face. She was beautiful, with pale skin and freckles across her cheeks. As if on cue she opened her eyes, her large dark pupils shrinking to pins at the intrusion of light, letting the emerald green irises glow as they focused on Danny.

'Mmm, are we dead?' she said groggily.

'Apparently not,' Danny said with a smile.

'Oh, good. Where are we?' she said, yawning as the remnants of the tranquilliser wore off.

'In the back of a lorry, heading for Manchester.'

'Ok. What? Manchester, how do you know?' she said, blushing as she realised she was hugging him.

Danny turned the light round and pointed as Alice sat up. There was a large delivery label on the pile of mattresses with Sleepwell, Manchester Store written on it.

'Can't we just call for help?' she said looking at his phone.

'Nope, we're inside a metal shipping container, no signal. We'll just have to wait until it stops and make a load of noise. Failing that, we're in here until they unload in Manchester.'

'Why didn't that guy kill us?' she said, rubbing her eyes.

'I have no idea,' Danny said placing the phone on the mattress and lying back down with his hands behind his head. 'Might as well make ourselves comfortable, we could be here for a while.'

Alice looked down at him with a coy smile. 'Well, I'm glad you're here with me,' she said, lowering herself down and kissing him unexpectedly.

Her lips were soft and warm and inviting. Danny found himself responding as he moved his arms around her. He ran his fingers through her long hair, feeling her lithe body as they embraced.

CHAPTER 58

Edward got into MI6 headquarters around half-six. Although suited as usual, after only two hours sleep the dark rings under the eyes and stubble shadow were a dead giveaway. When he entered the incident room, Howard greeted him from the coffee machine. He was wearing the same suit as yesterday, which led Edward to believe he'd been there all night. In contrast to Edward, Howard somehow looked as fresh as a daisy and mysteriously remained clean-shaven.

'Morning, Edward. The day of reckoning is amongst us, dear boy,' he said still upbeat.

'Quite. Anything new?'

'I'm afraid not. Scott cracked Hamish's laptop and found nothing of interest. He went home a little while ago. We do have a few traffic camera sightings of the ACM van on the night of the robbery before it disappears. They're on a primary route through London, leaving us with two options. One, they changed number plates and took the signage off, leaving London via one of six different directions. Or two, they delivered the device in London and hid the van,' said Howard, moving Edward over to two white-boards full of venue names.

'How does this help us?' said Edward puzzled.

'It doesn't, dear boy. I've had Logistics on it all night. We're in the middle of conference and event season and there are 148 possible targets countrywide. We have no way of covering all the venues and no discernible evidence to demand a national shutdown.'

'Basically, we're screwed then,' said Edward, rubbing his forehead.

'Not exactly my turn of phrase, but yes, we have a major problem. I have an emergency meeting at Central Hall with the Prime Minister, the Minister for Defence, and General Rufus McManus in a few hours. As much as it pains me to say so, I'm hoping the General has some insight that will help us. Anyway, I take it there's no news of Daniel?' Howard said, looking at Edward with a rare look of hopefulness.

'I'm afraid not. I think we have to assume the worst.'

'Mmm, I fear you may be right. What time does Christopher Swash get in?' Howard said, changing the subject.

'He should be here by seven thirty. Why are you so interested in Swash?' said Edward, puzzled at Howard's repeated interest in Swash.

'Because starting with Sergeant Simon Tripp's death, I get the constant feeling that parties unknown have been one step ahead of us all the way. And as far as I'm aware, no one other than the occupants of this department knew about Tripp or our visit to Hamish Campbell's place of residence. This would indicate to me that we have a leak in this department, wouldn't you agree?'

Edward pondered the question for a few seconds. 'Yes, I think it would.'

Moving quickly down the stairs into Edgware Road Tube Station, Christopher Swash tapped his Oyster card on the pad and hurried through the barriers. He made his way to the far end of the Circle line platform as he did every morning and stood near the edge on the yellow line. The train was quieter at the back. He waited for the next Tube, which the information board said would be in 2 minutes. His nerves were shot, and he could feel the acid in his stomach rising already. Reaching in his pocket, he pulled out a bottle of Gaviscon liquid and took a big swig.

Just a couple more days. Hold it together, the General will pay your debts and you can get on with your life.

Almost convincing himself, he felt a little better as the rumble of the approaching train echoed down the platform. The two lights came around the corner and the driver came into view sitting in his cab. What Christopher didn't see was the figure behind him, baseball hat pulled down low and hoodie pulled up over the top of it. When the Tube got within five metres of him, the figure stood close behind, his gloved hand hovering behind the base of Christopher's spine. A split-second later he was falling forward. There wasn't time to scream or comprehend his predicament—no sooner had he fallen, he thumped off the front of the train with a sickening dull thud and disappeared under it. He didn't know much about it. The impact knocked him unconscious before he was electrocuted by the third rail and crushed by the wheels. Screams rang out on the platform as the emergency brakes screeched and locked. The hooded figure was off the platform and out of the station before the train had ground to a halt.

CHAPTER 59

R ufus marched through the offices of Project Dragonfly. He was impeccably dressed in a Savile Row tailored navy suit. He'd had a haircut, shaved and picked the suit specially to celebrate this great day. It had been a tough mission, and he'd lost many good men, but his hour of glory was almost upon him. With the exception of Commander Benton, all loose ends were tied up. Benton could never go to the authorities; he'd be charged with multiple murders and knew Rufus would have him killed before he could do a deal. No, he'd leave the country; he was probably already gone.

There was nothing to lead back to him or Project Dragonfly. In two hours he would execute the most ambitious plan of his career. Once the PM, Pringle and Howard were removed, Anthony Burrows would take over as Prime Minister, Martin Trimley would be Minister for Defence, and Project Dragonfly would be re-commissioned as the UK's leading anti-terrorist unit. He walked to the front of the room with the rows of big screens and savoured the moment.

'Give me the internal feeds for the Central Hall, please,' Rufus said, more politely than the team was used to.

'And the street views,' he said pointing to the monitors to the left.

One by one the CCTV camera feeds from inside the building popped up until all twelve cameras were displayed on the central screens. Seconds later various images from outside of the building popped up from hacked nearby properties. The General smiled to himself at the sight of engineers setting up the microphones and podiums for the press conference in the Great Hall. On the outside cameras he spotted the plain-clothed security teams running their explosives-trained sniffer dogs through their final checks before securing the building.

'You won't find anything today, boys,' he whispered to himself, smug in the beauty of his planning.

He looked at his watch and checked his phone for the hundredth time for the number to trigger the pulse weapon.

Two hours to go. Patience, Rufus. Patience.

Spinning on his heels, he marched towards the canteen to get some coffee.

CHAPTER 60

With a new car and a new temporary driver, Howard approached the commotion surrounding Central Hall. He got the driver to drop him off around the corner from the venue and walked the rest of the way. Tucking in discreetly behind the press and media he flashed his ID to security as he entered the building. Uncomfortable in the presence of people he'd spent his entire career trying to remain anonymous from, Howard stood right at the back of the room. For the first time in a long time he was unsure of himself. He had days of terror and mayhem throughout the capital, there was a lethal weapon primed to go off somewhere in the country, and he had absolutely no evidence of who was behind it.

The Prime Minister appeared on the stage with Pringle by his side. Howard searched the stage and crowd for Rufus, but the General was nowhere to be seen. Perhaps he had booked one of the smaller rooms for the meeting and was waiting there. The Prime Minister addressing the crowd drew his attention back to the stage

CHAPTER 61

Despite their predicament Danny was feeling pretty good about things. Being drugged meant he'd slept well, nobody had tried to kill him for at least eight hours, he knew the location of the pulse weapon, and he'd met Alice. She was funny, sexy and interesting, and she brought out feelings in him he hadn't dared feel since an assassin known as the Chinaman killed his girlfriend a few years back.

They lay back and talked in the pitch black, to save the battery in his phone, for what seemed like an eternity. The steady engine noise and vibrations in the background suggested they were on the long drive up the motorway. Eventually the sound and movement changed; stops and starts and movement that had the two of them rolling from left to right. This could only mean the truck had entered the city and was closing in on its destination. Danny turned on the phone light to see Alice's smiling face lying beside him, blinking away the sudden intrusion of light.

'What's up?'

'I think we're getting close to the destination,' Danny

said as the lorry turned and stopped, then changed direction as it reversed.

'Come on,' Danny said standing. He reached down and took Alice's hand and pulled her up. Holding the light up in front of them, he squeezed and pulled Alice through the stacks of mattresses until they stood in the small gap between the loading door and its cargo of mattresses.

The seconds dragged by. Danny could hear faint voices outside which only made him more impatient. He needed to get out and call Edward, and he needed to do it now.

'Why don't we bang and shout?' said Alice, raising her fist.

Danny caught her arm and shook his head.

'If we do, they'll more than likely leave us in here and call the local plod to deal with us. By the time they get here, it could be too late.'

His patience paid off as the rattling and scraping of the container's metal doors sounded their imminent opening. When they did, Danny pushed them open, sending the tubby middle-aged lorry driver scurrying back in shock.

'Oi, who the hell are you? Asylum seekers? Stay there, I'm calling the police,' he said, growing in confidence as the store manager and warehouse lads appeared.

'Call them. Do it now, I need a lift back to London,' said Danny with a look they didn't want to mess with.

He turned away from them, pacing up and down in the loading bay as he waited for his phone to lock onto a signal. Finally the signal bars sprung into life, quickly followed by the pings of missed calls and messages from Edward, Howard and Scott. Ignoring them, Danny called Edward. He gave Alice a reassuring smile as he waited for it to connect.

'Jesus, Danny, where the hell have you been?' sounded a relieved Edward.

'Manchester. Don't ask. Listen carefully, Ed, the pulse weapon is at Central Hall, Westminster. You got it, Central Hall,' Danny said over all the chatter from the lorry driver and store staff.

'Shit. Howard and the Prime Minister are there for a press conference. I'll call you back,' said Edward, hanging up immediately.

Danny could picture Edward dialling as fast as he could while shouting orders across the incident room. He turned to look at the store manager. His eyes narrowed and his face set like granite while his muscular physique tensed. The little group in front of him went silent, not sure whether to challenge him or run.

'Have you called the police yet?' Danny growled slowly.

'I'm just... just about t—' the store manager said before Danny cut him short.

'I'll do it myself,' he said putting the phone to his ear.

CHAPTER 62

Howard's phone vibrated in his pocket. Sliding out of the hall, he pulled it out and answered.

'Howard, it's Rufus. I'm afraid I've been a little delayed. Are you there with the PM yet?' Rufus said, his tone unusually jovial.

'Yes, I'm here, the PM has moved on to the Q and A session from the press.'

'Excellent. Bear with me, I'll be there as soon as possible,' Rufus said hanging up without waiting for a reply.

'Damn,' said Edward when Howard's phone came up engaged. 'Tom, status,' he shouted across the room.

'Armed response is five minutes away. Bomb disposal twenty,' came Tom's shout over the agents on phones and bodies rushing about.

'Come on, come on, come on,' Edward mumbled to himself as he hit redial.

'Edward,' came Howard's welcome voice.

'Get everybody out, Howard. It's there, the pulse weapon, it's there at Central Hall. I've got officers en route, get out NOW!'

———

'Time to rid this country of these weak humanitarian do-gooders for the good of the country,' Rufus muttered to himself as he hit the dial button to trigger the pulse weapon. He moved his eyes up to the screens to watch the Prime Minister's Q and A and Howard on the phone in the corridor.

———

The screen on the pulse weapon lit up and the hydrogen power cells hissed as the reactor fired up.

'Is all good, shut it down,' said Miko Donovich to his technician.

The agent for the Russian Foreign Intelligence Service grinned excitedly. 'Excellent, you have done well, my friend. Russia thanks you,' he said turning to the lean Serbian standing next to him.

'As long as your thanks is worth three million euros, I accept,' he said, his inky black eyes holding their gaze with Miko's.

'Of course, your account details please,' said Miko smiling back unintimidated.

The Serbian gave him a piece of paper with the details on and watched as Miko repeated the details in Russian down the phone to his superiors.

'It is done,' he said, lowering the phone two minutes later.

The Serbian calmly got on his phone. He spoke in

English, offering identification details to the manager of the Grand Cayman bank. The faintest flicker of a smile curled up from the corner of his mouth as the transfer of funds was confirmed.

'A pleasure doing business with you, Mr Donovich.'

'Is no trouble, although it looks like you are no stranger to trouble, my friend,' Miko said pointing to the scars spreading from the Serbian's cheekbone across his face and down his neck.

'This? This is old. I got caught in an air strike in the troubles in Bosnia. I was lucky. An English Special Forces soldier pulled me out of the rubble and carried me on his back for two miles to a hospital. Saved my life,' he said touching the deep scars with his fingers.

'Lucky indeed. I guess you owe him a great debt,' said Miko as his technician finished securing the flight case on the pulse weapon.

'It is a debt that has recently been repaid. Goodbye, Miko, have a safe flight home,' he said, shaking hands before walking out of the aircraft hangar. He moved around the side of the Russian Antonov An-12 cargo plane to his motorbike. Taking the crash helmet off the handlebars, he paused as the phone in his pocket rang. Pulling it out with the tape and ribbon cable still attached, he answered it.

'Not today, General,' said The Hawk, calmly hanging up. He snapped the phone in two and threw it onto the tarmac. He put his helmet with the blacked-out visor on, fired up the powerful motorbike and sped away towards the exit gate.

———

Pulling the phone away from his ear, Rufus stared at it. He looked up at the screens. Everyone was alive and well and on the move. The Prime Minister and William Pringle were being led away by security staff, and Howard was co-ordinating the arrival of armed response officers to clear the building. He looked at the phone again, disbelief and confusion spinning around in his mind. As the seconds passed, his office techies looked at each other, then at the General, not knowing what to do next. As if hit by a bolt of lightning Rufus snapped back into life.

'Listen up, everyone. Enable the fire sale protocol. Let's go, people, burn the lot,' he bellowed across the room.

The room exploded into activity. People rushed to each terminal and typed in the confirmation code for the fire sale protocol aptly named after the fire damaged goods sale where everything must go. Hard drives and server files instantly wiped themselves, and the large screens at the front of the room started to go blank one after another. Rufus was on the phone again, walking away from his staff so he couldn't be overheard.

'I've just initiated the fire sale protocol. Your assistance is required,' he said heading for the lifts.

'We're on our way up, sir,' came the emotionless response.

Pushing through the heavy doors that led out of the office, Rufus moved into the stairwell and lift area. Four armed men dressed in black tactical body armour and balaclavas were there to meet him. The lead man nodded to Rufus as he walked past, leading his team into the office. The General walked up to the lift and calmly pressed the call button. He didn't flinch at the sound of suppressed automatic fire and the screams as his office staff were cut down. It was already justified in his mind; they knew too much and were collateral damage.

The game had changed. But he wasn't out yet.

CHAPTER 63

Showing his ID, Edward brushed past the police cordon and ducked the incident tape. He entered Central Hall, past the armed response and bomb disposal teams packing up their equipment, and headed for Howard.

'Anything, Howard?'

'The boys did a full sweep, the device isn't here,' said Howard, finally starting to look tired and stressed after the last couple of days.

'I can't understand it. Danny said it was in Hamish's folder.'

'I said the device *isn't* here, I didn't say it *wasn't* here.'

'Come again?' said Edward, puzzled.

'That middle-aged gentleman in the ill-fitting security uniform perfectly described Mendes and Knowles and the Transit van and a flight case the size of the pulse weapon. They delivered them on the night of its theft,' said Howard, pointing to the hall's security guard being interviewed by an MI6 agent.

'Well, if it was here, where the hell did it go?'

'That, Edward, is the million-dollar question. Where is Daniel anyway?' said Howard, frowning at the sight of General Rufus McManus entering the building.

'Somewhere on the M1. Manchester police are bringing him and Hamish's sister back as we speak.'

'Good, I need to talk to him once he's back. Would you excuse me a minute, Edward?' Howard said walking towards Rufus who was marching around the place like he was in charge.

'Rufus, good of you to show,' he said somewhat sarcastically.

'What the devil's been going on here then?' said Rufus, ignoring Howard's comment.

'We had a tip-off that the stolen pulse weapon was here and set to go off,' said Howard looking hard at Rufus, watching his body language and waiting to see his response.

'I take it from the lack of dead bodies, that isn't the case,' replied Rufus overly self-assured.

'It would appear not.'

'Well, bad luck old boy. I guess with Project Dragonfly being decommissioned, this mess falls squarely on your shoulders,' said Rufus, coming back with a newfound smugness.

The General turned to leave and started to walk away when Howard called after him.

'I spoke to the PM earlier. He had no knowledge of the emergency meeting.'

The General stopped in his tracks. He half-turned to look at Howard. 'Strange. I arranged it with his secretary, she must have made a mistake. Goodbye, Howard,' he said, marching out the door.

If Howard had been unsure of his suspicions before, he was certain they involved General Rufus McManus now.

CHAPTER 64

After a four-hour journey, Danny waved off the Manchester police officers at the reception of the SIS building. The twenty-four hours since he'd left there to go to Hamish's felt like a week ago. The closeness and feelings he had for Alice felt like a lifetime ago. Tom came down and greeted them. He signed them through security and escorted them upstairs to the incident room.

'What's been happening, Tom? Did you get to Central Hall in time? How many are dead?' Danny bombarded Tom with questions the moment they were away from reception.

'Wow, hold on, buddy, has nobody told you?'

'Told me what?' said Danny gruffly, his patience wearing thin.

'The pulse weapon wasn't there. No, wait. Let me rephrase that. The pulse weapon was there but someone removed it after the drop off,' replied Tom, holding the incident door open for Alice to walk through.

'What, but who? Fuck,' was all Danny managed to say.

Edward noticed them enter from the other side of the room and beckoned them over. The whiteboards had all changed since Danny had last seen them the day before. General Rufus McManus's photo was in the middle of the board, but there were no links to associate him with the suspects surrounding it.

'Who's the suit in the middle? His photo was in Hamish's folder.'

'That's the new prime suspect, General Rufus McManus, Senior Director of Project Dragonfly,' came Howard's voice from behind them.

'What? The special counter-terrorist unit. Why?'

'The usual reasons, power and money. The PM and Minister of Defence are shutting him down and it seems the General had other plans,' said Howard, moving to the front.

'Well, where is he? Have you arrested him?' said Danny in his usual impatient way.

'Ah, General Rufus McManus is a very careful man, Daniel. We have no proof, nothing.'

'But what about Benton and the men I killed in Stratford? The guys in the shopping centre, the one I knocked out in the changing rooms and the one the crowd jumped on?' said Danny frustrated by the way the conversation was going.

'The bodies are all gone, disappeared. Our unconscious friend in the changing rooms with a handgun nearby said nothing. An expensive solicitor turned up and had him released as there was no evidence to suggest the handgun was his. Ex-paratrooper Owen West was arrested and put in the holding cells at Stratford Police Station. They found him dead this morning, hanging in his cell by a length of mains flex. No visitors and the CCTV for the building went down for fifteen minutes at 3 a.m.'

'Shit, why is this guy on the board? I saw him in here the other day,' said Danny tapping the picture of Christopher Swash on the board.

'That is one of our agents. We had a suspicion he was giving information about our investigation to whoever was behind this. He was pushed under a Tube train on his way to work this morning,' said Edward joining the conversation.

Alice had been listening beside Danny. Her eyes flicked between the pictures on the board and the men as they ran through the dead ends. With all that had happened in the past couple of days, it took her a while to connect the dots. When she did, the anger welled up inside her.

'This bastard is the one who killed my brother and tried to kill me, and you're trying to tell me you can't do anything about it?' she yelled in frustration.

'I'm sorry, my dear, we just don't have any evidence,' said Howard, embarrassed that he couldn't offer her any hope of justice.

Alice's anger turned to emotion and tears welled up in her eyes. Danny turned to comfort her just in time for her to bury her head in his chest and sob uncontrollably. He put his arms around her and led her gently away. Howard turned to the board, gritted his teeth, and slammed his hand against it in anger. The move surprised Edward. It was the first time he'd seen Howard lose his composure in all the years he'd known him.

'Are you ok?' he asked softly.

'Yes, thank you, Edward. If you could just give me a minute,' Howard said quietly.

Edward nodded and left Howard to tend to his staff. Taking a deep breath, Howard composed himself. He straightened his suit and smoothed his hair into place. He was about to move away from the board when the photo of

Ivan and Nikolai Korentski caught his eye. Peeling it off the board, he stared at it long and hard. Sliding the photo into his suit jacket, he stared at the picture of Rufus. A small smile flickered across his face, visible for barely a second before he turned and moved confidently towards the exit.

'Take it all down, Edward, there's no case and the PM won't fund an investigation based on what little we know,' Howard said, storming out of the room without looking back.

'Ok,' Edward replied turning to see the doors swinging shut. A hand caught one and pushed it back open as Scott entered the room. He gave a big smile to Edward, who smiled back and pointed towards Danny standing with his back to them.

'Eh, I say, Daniel, old man,' came a voice Danny was glad to hear.

'Scotty boy, just the man I want to see,' he said, turning to look at Scott with a puffy-eyed Alice.

'Yes well, seeing as you carelessly got your house blown up, I thought I'd offer you the use of my other apartment. Oh hello, my dear,' Scott said spotting Alice.

'Scott, you're a lifesaver, thanks, man.'

'What do I do?' came a timid response from Alice.

Danny turned and looked at her. His face softened and he smiled reassuringly. 'I was kinda hoping you'd want to stay with me for a while.'

She reached up and put her hands around his neck. Her emerald eyes sparkled and she grinned before standing on tiptoe and kissing him passionately on the lips.

'I say, Daniel, very smooth, old man. Come on. My chariot awaits,' said Scott chuckling to himself.

CHAPTER 65

A week on from the Central Hall incident, General Rufus McManus walked briskly out of his office in Whitehall and turned into Marsham Street. Holding his back straight and head up in a parade ground manner, he moved through the general public with an air of disdain at their insignificance. Reaching his destination, he flashed his identification and entered the modern metal-clad facade of the Home Office building. Moving through the metal detector, Rufus checked the time on his watch as he picked it out of the x-ray machine tray along with his wallet, phone and change. When he reached the meeting room, he entered without knocking.

'Good morning, gentlemen,' he said loudly, taking the one seat set out to face the three men opposite.

'Good morning, Rufus,' said the Prime Minister, William Pringle and Howard in unison.

The meeting went swiftly. Howard was unusually quiet, answering only when required as William Pringle, the Minister for Defence, ran through the changeover from Project Dragonfly to Howard's covert intelligence services.

General Rufus McManus assisted in an overly confident manner. He looked smugly at Howard when the PM offered him a newly created position of Special National Security Adviser to the Cabinet as way of a consolation.

The agenda ticked by, papers were signed and the meeting came to an end. They all rose from their seats and went through the usual protocol of handshaking before departing. Howard hid his disgust for Rufus and shook his hand. Gripping Howard's tightly, Rufus leaned in and whispered in his ear.

'Prime ministers come and go, my friend, and when his time is up, I will finish what I started.'

Howard returned Rufus's grip with a vice-like one of his own and whispered back, 'Watch your back, General, the world is a dangerous place.'

They parted and smiled falsely at each other. They said their goodbyes in the presence of the PM and Pringle for appearances' sake, then left. Rufus was the first one out the front doors of the Home Office building. He marched off towards his office in Whitehall, he walked straight at pedestrians as he went, intimidating his inferiors to get out of his way.

Howard stood at the kerb and watched him go. A Range Rover Sport with blacked-out windows rolled smoothly to a stop beside him. Howard opened the rear door and got in.

'To my club, please, Frank.'

'Certainly, sir.'

'And Frank?'

'Yes sir?'

'It's good to have you back,' said Howard, smiling at the eyes looking at him in the rear-view mirror.

'It's good to be back, sir,' came Frank's reply.

Indicating, the Range Rover pulled smoothly out into

traffic. Fifty metres down the road, Howard's eyes burned through the one-way glass as they followed Rufus marching along the pavement.

'Is that him, sir?' said Frank from the front.

'It is indeed, Frank. It is indeed.'

CHAPTER 66

anny looked out the bedroom window of Scott's two-million-pound apartment, with its desirable views of the Thames and the skyscrapers of Canary Wharf beyond. He was sitting up in bed in one of Scott's way-too-small bathrobes with Alice snuggled in close beside him. She was tucking into tea and toast from a heavy silver tray; Danny's idea of a breakfast-in-bed treat.

'Mmm, I could get used to this,' she said patting his leg.

'Don't get too comfy, a couple more weeks and the builders will have my house back together and then we're out of here,' Danny said reaching over and pinching a slice of toast.

'Oi, this is my breakfast surprise. Soooo, what happens when we leave here?' she said, craning her head up to look at him.

'Well, I was thinking you might like to—' He stopped mid-sentence. The hairs on the back of his neck stood up and his entire body language changed. His face set like granite and his eyes were dark and alert. Alice started to say something, but Danny stopped her.

'Go to the bathroom and lock yourself in. Call Edward. Tell him to get someone down here now,' Danny said, already off the bed.

Alice wanted to ask what was going on, but the look on Danny's face was like the one at the shopping centre when they were being attacked. She got off the bed, grabbed the phone and locked herself in the en-suite bathroom. He'd heard the apartment door clicking shut, he was sure of it. The only other person with keys was Scott, and he didn't know the meaning of being quiet.

Looking around, Danny cursed the bathrobe and lack of weapons. He moved lightly to the door and peeped around it into the empty hall. Moving silently forward, he entered the open-plan kitchen and lounge area. Before he had a chance to move, Benton swung round from the small hall area inside the front door. He had a silenced Glock levelled at Danny's chest.

Benton was hardly recognizable. He had black rings under his sleepless, twitchy eyes, and there was heavy stubble on his face. His hand trembled badly as he pointed the gun.

'Take it easy Re—'

Before he could finish, Benton put two bullets into Danny's chest, knocking him off his feet and out of sight behind the kitchen island. Breathing erratically, Benton fought to get a grasp on reality. Danny's bathrobe had morphed in his mind, changing his appearance into that of his Afghan tormentor. Moving towards the island to check Danny was dead, Benton banged the side of his head with the handgun to clear the images away.

Darting his head around the worktop, he did a double-take at the sight of a thick silver serving tray with two bullet indentations. At the same time, Danny popped up from behind the far side of the island, swinging a rolling pin like a baseball bat. It struck Benton's gun hand with a heavy crack, knocking the Glock flying into the lounge. He followed it up with a swing at Benton's head, but his reactions were too fast. Benton threw his forearm up to block the swing and hammered a blow into Danny's ribs. There was a crack followed by a searing pain as the rib fractured.

Crumpling to one side, Danny left himself open to a left hook to the side of his head. Struggling to keep upright, Danny shoved his hand up in Benton's crotch, gripping his family jewels with all his might. Ignoring the pain in his side, he lifted Benton off the ground and charged forward, slamming him down onto the kitchen worktop. Letting out a painful grunt, Benton stared at Danny with a crazy, glazed-over look in his eyes. His face went crimson as he fought for breath.

True to their training, they both lived by the same rules. When your lives are on the line, you fight and keep on fighting. Benton dug deep and kneed Danny in his fractured ribs, causing him to stagger back in agony. They both slowly stood at either end of the kitchen, their eyes locking across the small space.

Benton was sucking in great gulps of air to control the pain in his groin; Danny stood with one hand on the kitchen work surface to steady himself. He breathed heavily, waiting for the white-hot pain in his side to subside.

The seconds felt like hours until Benton finally broke the deadlock by reaching down and sliding a 6-inch commando knife out of its sheath. In mirrored synchronicity, Danny reached over and slid a carving knife out of the block on the kitchen worktop. They both held their arms up at shoulder height, tense and prepared as they advanced inch by inch.

When it happened it was explosive, metal on metal as they jabbed, slashed and blocked each other. With every block, they'd try to get a punch or a kick or knee in at each other. Benton's razor-sharp serrated knife sliced through Danny's floppy dressing gown sleeve, slicing deeply into the palm of his knife hand. The electric shock of pain as the blade hit nerve endings caused Danny to drop the carving knife. It clattered to the ground between them as they parted back to either side of the kitchen. They stood for a second, blood pouring from Danny's clenched fist as it ran down his arm.

Round two came fast. Benton lunged forward, the knife in front of him. Danny ducked to one side and grabbed the stainless-steel kettle, powering it—water and all—into Benton's head, knocking him sideways. Keeping on the attack, Danny planted his bare foot into Benton's middle, kicking him clean out of the kitchen to land on his back in the lounge. Adrenaline overriding the pain from his broken ribs, Danny jumped on top of Benton, gripping the wrist of his knife hand to push it away. Still holding the dented kettle, Danny went to batter Benton around the head with it. Instead of shying away, Benton threw his head forward and headbutted it away with a manic grin on his face. He followed it up with another crushing blow to Danny's broken rib, bending it inwards to puncture his lung.

Danny collapsed to the floor in agony, unable to breathe. Looking up, all he could see was Benton's crazed face looking down at him. His eyes were distant and he was muttering something in Arabic or Afghan Farsi. He raised the commando knife, holding it in two hands with the blade pointing down, ready to plunge it into Danny's heart.

Injured, breathless and weak, there was nothing Danny could do to stop him. He felt a strange calmness come over him, the acceptance of the fate he'd always known would get him one day. As he watched the blade coming down in mind-altered slow motion, Benton's body jerked and shook as he coughed a great plume of blood out of his mouth and nose-dived to the floor beside him. Alice stood in Benton's place holding his silenced Glock, smoke still rising from its barrel, making her pale, shocked face hazy. She dropped the gun and rushed to his side.

'I thought I told you to stay in the bathroom,' Danny wheezed as he tried and failed to sit up.

'Yeah and look where that got you,' she bit back, diving to her knees and cradling his head.

'Thank fuck you didn't listen to me,' Danny said chuckling and instantly regretting it.

'Just lie still, help's on the way.'

Right on cue, the front door burst inward as armed police and MI6 poured into the apartment. They took a second to secure the scene before Edward and the paramedics came in.

'You two ok? No bullet wounds?' Edward said, rushing to their side.

'No bullet wounds, but do I look fucking alright? Why do you lot always turn up after I get injured? Just for once it'd be nice if you turned up before someone tries to kill me,' Danny said in wheezy gasps as paramedics knelt either side of him unzipping their kit bags.

'Yeah, he's alright,' Edward chuckled.

He looked at Alice in her dressing gown. 'Do you want to get dressed, Alice? You can go with him to the hospital. I'll take care of everything here,' he said helping her up.

She nodded and padded barefoot to the bedroom, shutting the door to change.

'Looks like you've got a good one there,' he said winking at Danny.

Danny groaned as the paramedics slid him onto a stretcher, pulling it up to waist height so they could wheel him out. In a flash Alice was at his side, dressed in jeans and a jumper with her hair scooped up into a big, curly, red ponytail. She held his hand and looked down at him with gorgeous emerald eyes and a perfect smile.

Danny turned to Edward and smiled through the pain.

'You're right about that one. Thanks, Ed.'

CHAPTER 67

Upstairs in his London townhouse, General Rufus McManus looked at his Rolex. He wandered over to the white painted sash windows and looked down on the street below. His black Range Rover pulled in outside his house, parking perfectly straight, its wheels six inches off the kerb.

Bang on time as always, Hugh. Good man.

Sliding his suit jacket on, he adjusted his tie in the mirror and stood back to admire himself.

Those idiots will have to get up damn early in the morning to put one over on me.

He danced light-footed down the stairs and opened the front door. After locking it behind him he stopped at the top of the three white steps to the pavement. Looking down his nose, he waited for a group of scruffy students to pass by before he proceeded to the car. Opening the door, he slid onto the big leather rear seat.

'To the club please, Hugh,' he said, only looking up after he'd checked his watch.

'I don't think so, General,' said Ivan Korentski turning

around in the front passenger seat, a silenced Glock in his hand.

'Who the hell are you?' Rufus ordered, outraged by the intrusion and only just noticing the huge bulk of Gregor Krulsh in the driving seat.

Ivan smiled as Gregor eased the Range Rover into traffic.

'I am Ivan Korentski. You had my brother Nikolai killed in the port of Durrës,' said Ivan, his face devoid of emotion.

'The Russian gunrunners. What do you want, money?' growled Rufus, talking to Ivan with a dismissive arrogance.

'No, no, General, this is not about money. This is about avenging my brother's death.'

'Mr Korentski, everything is about money. Now name your price,' said Rufus, keeping calm.

'I have a message to give you from a mutual friend of ours. He said the world is a dangerous place, General, you should watch your back.'

The General's face went white as a sheet as the penny dropped and the gravity of his predicament sunk in.

'Whatever that bastard Howard paid you, I'll double it. I could use a couple of good men like you,' said Rufus, his arrogance still making him think he could turn this around.

'You did use us, you dumb fuck. You used us then killed my brother and tried to kill me. There's not enough money in the world to save you now. I'm going to hurt you, General. I'm going to hurt you so bad you're going to beg me to kill you.'

The General's mind started racing as he tried to think of a way out.

'You kill me, and my men will hunt you down like dogs. Stop this now and you can still come out of this on top.'

'Ha, this stupid motherfucker still doesn't get it, Ivan,'

said Gregor, his eyes cutting into Rufus in the rear-view mirror.

Ivan tilted the gun down slightly and pulled the trigger. The bullet shattered Rufus's kneecap, ripping the joint apart before lodging in the bone. The General howled in pain. He rolled around on the back seat clutching his knee, the cream leather smearing a bright red with slippery blood.

'He gets it now, Gregor,' said Ivan to his loyal friend.

'For Nikolai,' Gregor said.

'Yes, for Nikolai.'

CHAPTER 68

The Russian Ural-4320 army truck rumbled through Moscow. It had an armoured Typhoon 4x4 escort front and back. At the end of its forty-minute journey from Chkalovsky military air base, it pulled up at a top-secret military facility. The armed guards were expecting them, saluting as they opened the gate. Moving to the rear of the building, the truck backed up to a loading bay where a group of army officials were waiting. As Miko Donovich climbed down from the truck, Colonel Stephan Aliyev approached him, all smiles and a hand out to greet him.

'Miko, it's good to see you.'

'Thank you, Colonel, it's good to be home,' Miko said shaking his hand.

'Is that it?' the Colonel said, pointing at the flight case being fork-lifted off the truck.

'Yes, Colonel.'

'Excellent, excellent, you will get a commendation for this,' said Stephan gleefully.

'Thank you,' said Miko as they watched the forklift disappear into the cavernous facility.

It drove down one of the aisles between the floor-to-ceiling racks full of crates and boxes and devices of war, finally turning on the spot to raise its forks high in the air. With well-practiced skill, the driver placed the flight case gently down on the top shelf. He lowered the forks and drove away. Parking the forklift he headed for the exit door, with the twist of an industrial switch he plunged the warehouse into darkness as he left.

CHAPTER 69

'Are you sure you're up to this, old man?' said Scott from the driving seat of his Porsche.

'I'd feel a whole lot better about it if you'd brought a car I can actually get in and out of,' said Danny from the passenger seat, holding his painful side as Scott powered the car around.

'You didn't complain when you were squeezed in the back with one of the Minelli twins,' replied Scott with a chuckle.

'Oh yeah, and who are the Minelli twins?' said Alice, her face appearing between the seat as she leaned forward.

'Just ignore him, he's being an idiot,' said Danny turning to face her.

Alice's eyes sparkled. She gave a grin that would light up a dark room, then moved in and kissed him.

'Good God, can't you two give it a rest for more than a minute?' said Scott tapping the brakes a little too hard, sending Alice falling back into her seat behind them.

'Oops, sorry, my dear,' Scott said with a chuckle.

'You're an arsehole,' said Danny laughing then holding his side as his healing ribs grumbled.

'What's the matter, Scott, are you feeling left out?' Alice said from the back.

'Definitely not, my dear. The last time I was that loved-up the divorce cost me a small fortune and a very nice house. I think I'll stick to my shallow, self-indulgent little affairs if you don't mind. Oh, hang on, we're here,' said Scott pulling up outside Danny's house.

It was still surrounded by scaffolding, and the render needed painting, but apart from that the house looked pretty intact. Scott got out first, folding the seat forward and lending a hand for Alice to climb out of the back. They both moved round to the passenger door and tried to help Danny as he painfully climbed out of the low seat.

'I'm ok, don't fuss, I'll do it,' he said gruffly.

'Alright, caveman, get yourself out then,' said Scott turning away to look at the house.

After much huffing and puffing, Danny was up and next to them.

'Sorry,' he finally said.

'Apology accepted,' Alice said taking his hand and smiling up at him.

'I don't know why we're bothering to come over here now, the house is back together but everything inside was ruined. I've got to get carpets and furniture and a new kitchen before we can move back in.'

'Oh, come on. I just want to see it,' said Alice, dragging him up to the new front door.

'Ok, ok,' said Danny reaching into his pocket to pull out the shiny new keys the insurance company had sent him.

Stepping into the hall, Scott shut the door behind them. Danny's senses tingled and alarm bells rang in his head. There was someone else in the house, he could feel it. He stepped in front of Alice, clenching his fist as he prepared himself for attack. Slowly, he opened the living room door.

'Surprise!' came the shouts from his brother Rob and his wife Tina.

His three-year-old niece, Sophie, toddled towards him with her arms wide as she giggled excitedly.

Scooping her up on his good side, Danny smiled despite the pain and hugged her as she put her arms around his neck.

'What's all this in aid of?' he said, noticing the carpet, furniture and large TV for the first time. 'Where'd all this come from?'

'Courtesy of Her Majesty's Government for services rendered,' came a voice from behind him.

Danny turned to see Edward and Tom.

'Don't look at me, Howard sorted it all out. Living room, kitchen the lot. Have a look,' said Edward moving aside.

Danny put Sophie down, he moved along the hall and entered the kitchen with its new shiny cupboards and granite worktop. He opened the big American-style fridge, surprised to see it fully stocked, complete with an ample supply of beer. He turned to look at Alice, grinning.

'Anyone fancy a beer?' he shouted.

ABOUT THE AUTHOR

Stephen Taylor was born in 1968 in Walthamstow,
London.

I've always had a love of action thriller books, Lee Child's
Jack Reacher and Vince Flynn's Mitch Rapp and Tom
Wood, Victor. I also love action movies, Die Hard, Daniel
Craig's Bond and Jason Statham in The Transporter and
don't get me started on Guy Richie's Lock Stock or Snatch.
The harder and faster the action the better, with a bit of
humour thrown in to move it along.

The Danny Pearson series can be read in any order. Fans
of Lee Child's jack Reacher or Vince Flynn's Mitch Rapp
and Clive Cussler novels will find these books infinitely
more fun. If you're expecting a Dan Brown or Ian Rankin
you'll probably hate them.

www.ingramcontent.com/pod-product-compliance
Lightning Source LLC
LaVergne TN
LVHW031457020525
810239LV00027B/169